# IN FOR
# THE KILL

# PAULINE
# ROWSON

Fathom

IN FOR THE KILL
First published in 2007 by Fathom

Fathom is an imprint of Rowmark Publishing Limited
65 Rogers Mead
Hayling Island
Hampshire
England
PO11 0PL

ISBN: 978-0-9550982-2-2

Copyright © Pauline Rowson 2007

The right of Pauline Rowson to be identified as the author of this work has been asserted by her in accordance with the Copyright, Designs and Patents Act 1988.

All rights reserved. No part of this publication may be reproduced in any material form (including photocopying or storing it in any medium by electronic means and whether or not transiently or incidentally to some other use of publication) without the written permission of the copyright owner except in accordance with the provisions of the Copyright, Designs and Patents Act 1988 or under the terms of a licence issued by the Copyright Licensing Agency Ltd. 90 Tottenham Court Road, London, England W1P 9HE. Applications for the copyright owner's written permission to reproduce any part of this publication should be addressed to the publisher.

Warning: The doing of an unauthorised act in relation to a copyright work may result in both a civil claim for damages and criminal prosecution.

This novel is entirely a work of fiction. The names, characters and incidents portrayed in it are entirely the work of the author's imagination. Any resemblance to actual persons, living or dead, events or locations is entirely coincidental.

Printed in Great Britain by J. H. Haynes & Co. Ltd., Sparkford

Fathom is an imprint of Rowmark Limited

## PAULINE ROWSON

Pauline Rowson was raised in Portsmouth and is a frequent visitor to the Isle of Wight, the setting for this marine mystery thriller. In addition to being a crime writer she is the author of several marketing, self-help and motivational books. She lives in Hampshire and can never be far from the sea for any length of time without suffering withdrawal symptoms. This is her third marine mystery and she plans many more…

**Praise for *Tide of Death* featuring DI Andy Horton and his sidekick Barney Cantelli**

'Rowson manages to mix criminal and maritime worlds into a fast paced thriller, from police stations to Bavaria yachts the reader is fixed.' *Julian Gowing, Opal Marine.*

'With the Harley Davidson riding Horton living on a yacht and the various harbours and marinas around Portsmouth playing a major part in the action this is ideal reading - just check out that yacht in the next berth.' *Sail-World.com*

'If you are looking for a gripping read, to while away the time between sailing, try murder mystery *Tide of Death*.' *Yachts and Yachting Magazine*

'Rowson's marine mystery series can do for the Solent what Inspector Morse did for Oxford.' *Daily Echo*

'Hoist the sails for DI Andy Horton and his sidekick Barney Cantelli. A series with a fair wind behind it and destined to go far.' *Amy Myers*

'A detective novel with a cutting edge. A great marine mystery with action.' *Marine Update*

**Reader Reviews for *Tide of Death***

'Marvellous! A detective story that kept me enthralled to the end.'

'This is the first detective crime novel I have read and I thoroughly enjoyed it. Can't wait to read the next one!'

'Andy Horton is great. Can't wait to find out what happens to him in the next book.'

'Pauline Rowson has combined the glamorous yachting world on the south coast with the seedy criminal world in a fast moving, easy to read marine mystery. The reader is transported straight into the world of deception and intrigue. I could not put this book down. It is a must read.'

**Praise for *In Cold Daylight* – A Marine Mystery fast paced thriller**

'Twists and turns described this perfectly. I enjoyed it and couldn't put it down. Can't wait for the next one. I'm hooked.'

'I really enjoyed this. It kept me turning the pages.'

'Great! I was up until 3am to finish this.'

'This is a fast-paced and enjoyable book with many twists and turns. The characters are well defined and the plotting is excellent. For the reader who likes an atmospheric novel together with a good mystery, Rowson is one to watch.'
*www.reviewingtheevidence.co.uk*

*For Jackie*

*Mine honour is my life: both grow in one;*
*Take honour from me, and my life is done.*

**Richard II Act 1. Scene 1.**

# PROLOGUE

*April*

There is before and after, like one of those slimming adverts you see in magazines and newspapers. Only my before and after had nothing to do with diet, unless you counted prison food. Before prison I had been confident and successful. I had a family and a career. I had friends. And after? Well, here I am standing outside Camp Hill on the Isle of Wight getting high on the smell of diesel and petrol fumes, hesitant, with a prison pallor and a prison stoop.

For forty-two months, one week and two days I had dreamt of this moment. Now that it had arrived I felt a flutter of panic that almost had me scurrying back to the gates of Camp Hill pleading to be allowed back in. Goodness knows what lifers must feel!

'Hey, Alex! Over here.'

I pulled myself together and headed towards the black Mercedes. Remember who you once were I said to myself. But that Alex Albury had vanished one September when, in the early hours of the morning, the police had burst into my home on the Hamble and had arrested me for something I hadn't done.

I climbed into the waiting car and glanced at my defence lawyer. Miles gave me a brief nod before pulling out into the traffic. We didn't speak. As the prison receded my breathing became easier. My pulse settled down and I felt the tension drain from my body. As we climbed Brading Down, the sparkling blue of the Solent in the distance stole the breath from my body.

It was then that I knew no matter what the cost I would find James Andover. I would ask him why he had framed me. And then I would destroy him as he had destroyed me.

# Chapter 1

'To freedom and the future.' Miles Wolverton peered at me over the rim of his glass.

Chink. I swallowed and pulled a face. I'd forgotten how dry champagne is. I stared around my immaculately clean houseboat, courtesy of Miles's cleaning lady, Angela. It didn't seem real. This was a dream and at any moment I would wake up and find myself back in my cell.

'So what now?' Miles asked, easing himself down on the blue and white striped cushioned bench that ran either side of my narrow lounge.

He stretched out his short legs, eyeing me curiously with those green penetrating eyes that I had seen so often across the courtroom and in the prison visitors' centre. I thought how out of place he looked in his pin-striped suit. And, to me, his broad physique, bull neck and rugged face made him much more a candidate for the building site than the law courts. I hadn't wanted him to meet me from prison; I would have preferred to be alone, but Miles had meant well. I guess he still felt guilty for not getting me off the charges of fraud and embezzlement.

I turned to stare out of the patio doors at a scene I had dreamt of so many times in my prison cell. The tide was rushing out of Bembridge Harbour, carrying with it a small yacht, its sails as yet unfurled, its diesel engine chugging gently. To my right, on the curving sandy beach, a woman was throwing a ball into the sea for a liver and white spaniel.

'Now I find the truth,' I said, quietly.

'Alex, it's over. Put it behind you and move on.'

I spun round. 'Move on? Where? Doing what?'

'You can work for us.'

I gazed at him disbelievingly.

'I've told your probation officer and I've squared it with my partners.'

'I can't –'

'You don't even have to come to the mainland for the partners' meetings. I can get our marketing manager to e-mail anything that's required and you can start by writing some press releases and articles for us.'

'No.'

'You needn't start right –'

'Miles, you don't understand. How can I go back to being a PR man when my reputation has been destroyed? Andover's still out there somewhere and I have to find him – whoever he is – otherwise how do I know that he won't frame me again? And I need to know why he hated me enough to have me convicted for five years.'

I poured myself another glass of champagne, but didn't drink it. I'd finally been given parole two-thirds of the way through my sentence. I'd had to tell the parole board that I was sorry I had swindled three prominent businessmen out of one million pounds each, and admitted that Andover had been my partner and had absconded with the money.

'*Words,*' my cellmate, Ray, had said, '*mean nothing. Only action counts.*'

Well, now *I* was going to take some action and it wasn't finding myself a job. I had some money from the sale of my mother's house on her death and the houseboat was in my name. It wasn't much, but it was enough to keep me going until I got to the truth. Or, at least, I hoped it was.

Miles shifted his squat body and scowled at me. 'I don't think the parole board will like it.'

'Then we'll just have to keep it from them,' I replied sharply, and then almost instantly relented. It was hardly Miles's fault. He'd done his best to keep me out of prison.

'What if you never find Andover?'

'Then I'll die a bitter, frustrated man.'

'I understand what you must be feeling, but –'

'You don't!' I rounded on him. 'How can you? You haven't lost your wife and your children, your home, your future, your reputation, your freedom. You've lost nothing. I've lost everything, even my sodding confidence.'

My words fell into a pool of silence. I stared at the photograph on the narrow shelf behind the bench seat. My sons smiled back at me, their hair ruffled by the wind, their faces tanned, red lifejackets swamping their small chests. The picture had been taken on my boat during our last holiday before my arrest. David was aged ten then, dark-haired and two years older than Philip. God, how I missed them!

A tight band gripped my chest and I pushed back the patio doors and stepped onto the deck, trying to catch my breath. An unseasonably warm

April breeze caressed my face, bringing with it the smell of seaweed and sand. A large white butterfly settled for a moment on the guardrail, opened its wings and then took off again. I followed it with eyes that were moist and a lump in my throat the size of a golf ball. Before prison I wouldn't have noticed it if it had perched on the end of my nose!

I took a few deep breaths and told myself that big men don't cry, but my heart had been weeping since the day they had taken away my freedom.

Miles's voice came quietly from just behind me. 'I let you down, Alex. I should have found a way to get you off, or at least get you a community sentence, but your trial came at the wrong time.'

Yes, January is always a dry month for news. And I had to be made an example of, the PR man who had swindled three respected businessmen. It was a good story.

I turned to face Miles. 'You did your best.'

'And it wasn't good enough.'

No, it wasn't.

'Joe Bristow couldn't trace Andover and neither could the police, so how can you?' he asked.

Joe had been the private investigator that Miles had hired on my behalf. He had stopped looking for Andover just over a year ago. Joe had told me

to save my money. As far as he was concerned
Andover had flown.

'I have to try,' I said.

Miles sighed in capitulation. He saw that he
wasn't going to get me to change my mind. 'If
there's anything I can do to help find him just
say the word.'

Before I could answer his mobile phone rang.
Miles went inside to take his call.

My mind trawled through the events of my
arrest and trial, just as it had done a thousand
times before. Each time I hoped for some clue
that could tell me why Andover had framed me
and each time I drew a blank.

It had started long before my arrest. Six years
ago James Andover had set up a registered charity
to raise money to research into the causes of heart
disease. Andover had named himself, me and two
other businessmen as his fellow trustees. He had
complied with all the regulations of the Charity
Commission and filled in the forms. Then he
had targeted three men: Couldner, Westnam and
Brookes, all of whom had donated over a two-
year period the sum of one million pounds each.
The money had gone into the charity bank
account, and then into another bank account in
my name, only I hadn't opened it. The money
had then been transferred, all electronically

without me even being aware of it. Where it was now I had no idea, though the police had thought differently. When Couldner had died in a car accident in the May before my arrest, his daughter had become suspicious over her father's dwindling bank account and reported it to the police. They had traced it to the charity and hence to me. Andover had disappeared, and the other trustees had proved to be fictitious, names taken from gravestones, signatures forged. The registered office of the charity had been my mother's house in Bembridge. A divert had been put on the mail though, to another address which was an empty one-room office in the middle of London, registered in my name. The two surviving businessmen, Roger Brookes and Clive Westnam, swore they had been contacted by me and had donated money in good faith. I was left as the one tangible person to carry the can.

I'd never heard of the charity and neither had I ever been a trustee. Of course the police didn't believe that; not with the overwhelming evidence they uncovered. The Hi Tech Crime Unit had also discovered deleted e-mails from me to Andover on my computer hard drive. I hadn't sent them. No one believed me. They were on the computer therefore it had to be true. Computers didn't lie. Humans did. I'd since discovered that a computer hacker could easily have hacked into my computer via the Internet and put them there.

'I've got to go,' Miles said, interrupting my thoughts. 'Crisis with a client. Will you be all right?'

'I'll be fine,' I replied, trying to hide my relief. 'Thanks for the lift and the champagne.'

'You sure you don't want to come over to Portsmouth? You can stay with me.'

'No. Thanks.' Company was the last thing I needed after sharing my life with almost six hundred men.

Miles opened the boot of his car and reached for a mauve folder. 'The press cuttings you asked for.'

'Are they all there?'

'Yes.'

He looked as if he wanted to ask me why I needed them. It wasn't to start a scrapbook.

I watched the Mercedes glide towards St Helens, past a black van with tinted windows parked on the slipway. It was the same van that had followed us across Brading Down. I wasn't sure if it had been behind us before then. It could just be a coincidence, but I was edgy. What if the police were watching me? I didn't want them dogging my footsteps in my search for Andover.

And I didn't want them anywhere near me when I found him.

I wouldn't have put it past DCI Clipton to have me tailed. He'd never believed in my innocence. How I hated that man for the torment he had put me through. My conviction had been a feather in his cap, a step up to Detective Superintendent, and head of the Specialist Investigations Unit in south Hampshire. Well, I hoped his workload was so huge that it gave him sleepless nights and ulcers. If he had detailed someone to keep an eye on me, then somehow I would have to shake him off.

I put the press cuttings file on the houseboat, pushed a baseball style cap low over my face to avoid being recognised by any of the villagers, and went back out into the sunshine. It was too good a day to waste and I needed to stretch my legs.

At the end of the Embankment I ducked down onto the beach by the Toll Gate café, where a handful of holiday-makers were sitting at the wooden picnic benches making the most of the April sun, and I struck out along the beach. I resisted the urge to remove my trainers and socks and feel the soft sand between my toes. I would save that pleasure for another day just as I would the sensation of cold seawater on my feet and body. Now I simply delighted in hearing sounds that had been lost to me for so long: the calling of the seagulls, the gentle ripple of the sea as it rolled onto the shore, and the rustle of the breeze through the trees as I stepped up onto the coastal path. I nodded at the occasional dog walker but didn't meet anyone I recognised. I removed my cap and lifted my head higher.

Soon I was striding across Bembridge Airfield on my way to Brading, feeling the sun on my back and the gentle breeze on my face. I thought I was in heaven. But I couldn't relax, not with Andover hanging over me.

Why had Couldner, Westnam and Brookes given so generously and willingly? Why had Andover chosen *them* as victims? There had to be a reason, some kind of connection between them, and I had to find it. There had been no hint at my trial that they had been blackmailed by Andover, even though my barrister had put it to Westnam and Brookes. *I* knew they had, because I knew I was innocent. All three men couldn't have been so modest that they hadn't wanted their donations to be made public! Whatever Andover had threatened them with it had to be something big enough for them to pay up and then remain silent when questioned under oath. Joe Bristow hadn't discovered it, though he had dug deep into their affairs, I might not either, but I had to try.

I pushed back the door to Brading church and found myself face to face with a vision of such beauty that she made me go weak at the knees. Embarrassingly I found myself blushing, something I hadn't done since a teenager. I guessed she was in her early twenties. Her legs seemed to stretch up into infinity and her shoulder length hair was so thick and golden that it reminded me of a field of ripe corn. Despite my best efforts at self-control my body responded to three and a half years of enforced celibacy. I cleared my throat and tried to speak but the words wouldn't come. If she noticed my discomfort she didn't show it. Instead she smiled and said:

'It's incredible that there was once an Anglo-Saxon village here, right where we are standing.'

I think I mumbled something in reply, but wouldn't swear to it. I felt like a bloody adolescent schoolboy.

'I'm a historian,' she added, apparently undaunted by my silence. 'I get carried away sometimes, occupational hazard. I think I live more in the past than the present and that's not very healthy.'

Tell me about it I thought, her words striking a chord with me. Had she just given me a message: stay away from the past, from Andover, or else? No, that was ridiculous.

'Are you researching the church's history?' I finally found my voice. I was curious about her.

'No. I'm writing a book about the Island during the Second World War.'

'That shouldn't take you long,' I said jokingly. The Island was very small, only twenty-three miles from east to west and just over thirteen miles from north to south. Its population of about a hundred and twenty thousand increased by many in the summer holiday season. I didn't know much about the part the Island had played during the war, apart from the tales Percy Trentham used to spout about the radar station. I hadn't really been interested.

'On the contrary,' she said, 'The Island is most fascinating and the past can often help us put things into perspective. We're all so self-obsessed with our own petty problems today, and yet in a hundred years' time we'll all be dead and what we thought so important will be forgotten.'

'It's a point of view.'

'And one you don't share?' She gazed at me curiously. I saw amusement in her sapphire blue eyes.

'No,' I replied. My problems were important now because I had to live now and not in the past or the future. Someone other than myself had rewritten my future because he had radically altered my past. I had to know why. I had to set the record straight not only for myself but more importantly for the future of my boys, and their children.

She looked as if she wanted to challenge me, but something in my expression must have made her reconsider.

Abruptly she said, 'Well, I mustn't disturb you.'

With a smile she was gone. The church felt cold and dark after she had left as though she had taken the sunshine with her. I closed the heavy oak door behind me annoyed with myself for being so inept. The smooth-talking easy-going Alex Albury had evaporated over the last few years, leaving a tongue-tied idiot in his place.

As I walked back across the marsh and through the woods to Bembridge I examined her words. It was as though there were a subtext to her conversation. Was it some kind of warning? Or was I just being paranoid? I couldn't be blamed for having a persecution complex. Perhaps she really was a historian and the meeting pure coincidence. I had to get a grip on myself. I couldn't see suspicion everywhere I looked.

I had reached the airfield again when I heard the throb of an engine behind me. I glanced over my shoulder and saw that a light aircraft was just coming into land. I picked up my pace. I had time to reach safety.

The aeroplane throttled back. I looked again in its direction, more anxiously this time. It seemed to be approaching with alarming speed. I walked faster, but it was getting nearer. It was closing rapidly on me. Jesus!

I broke into a run cricking my neck over my shoulder. It was heading straight for me. Couldn't the bloody idiot see me? But then my blood ran cold, of course he could. I was the prey.

I swerved but still it came. The sweat was pouring down my face. My breath was coming in hisses and gasps. My feet were striking against the hard hummocky turf. Desperately I tried to keep my balance, the uneven surface jarring my knees and twisting my ankles. The hedgerow and safety seemed as far away as ever.

Suddenly the throb of the engine was in my ears, inside my head. It was so loud that it must be on top of me. I dropped to the ground flattening my face in the wet grass. It swooped over me with a roar, almost brushing my hair. I didn't have a moment to lose, certainly not to lie here panting. I sprang up and tore across the remaining strip of grass.

The aeroplane was flying in the direction of

the harbour across the bird sanctuary. It dipped its wings as it turned. It was coming back, but I would be out of its reach by then. Already my calf muscles were telling me I was climbing the hill to the windmill and safety. The pilot must have seen this because the aeroplane turned round and headed out to sea.

I walked quickly back through the village and along the Embankment, hoping I wouldn't see anyone I knew. My head was spinning with what had just happened. Had the pilot intended killing me? It would have been a clumsy way to do so and would probably have resulted in his own death. I didn't think even the most desperate of men would commit suicide over me. But why attempt to frighten or injure me? The answer was simple; it was a warning, just like that woman's in the church. Forget the past. Do nothing and you'll be allowed to live. But doing nothing wasn't a choice I had. No amount of warnings was going to frighten me off. I had been out of prison less than twelve hours and already Andover was running scared. That was good.

I let myself into the houseboat feeling optimistic. Joe Bristow had been wrong. Andover hadn't flown the country. He was right here in England, perhaps even on the Isle of Wight. Now all I had to do was find him.

# CHAPTER 2

I rose early the next morning after a restless night. The houseboat had seemed eerily quiet; I had missed the sound of men snoring and coughing, the prison warders' footsteps along the corridors, the slamming of doors and the rattling of keys.

I took a quick shower unable to adjust to the fact that I could stay as long as I wanted under scalding hot water. Then, after sitting with a coffee and watching the sun rise over the harbour, I stirred myself and took a long walk around the shore to Culver Cliff. Here I looked out upon the world. The sea sparkled and shimmered beneath me in the crisp, April morning, but instead of making me feel happy it had the opposite effect. My heart was once again heavy with the thought of all the mornings I had lost at the hand of Andover. I couldn't feel at peace with myself. Andover and the poison of prison had seeped its way into my soul and had made everything sour. Time to do something. The world would have woken up by now I thought, consulting my watch.

Bembridge library was open. The librarians were busy with a couple of grey haired women who looked vaguely familiar, my mother's old friends I seemed to recall. I scuttled past them, my head low, cursing Andover silently for forcing me to behave like this. One day, I vowed, I would hold my head up high and not feel ashamed.

I looked up Clive Westnam on the Internet and found references in various articles to my court case and the embezzlement. There didn't seem to be anything I hadn't read before, and certainly nothing that wasn't already in Joe's reports, which I had studied again last night. The references seemed to stop about two years ago. That had been when three judges had ruled that my sentence would stand. It was the second and final time they had refused my leave to appeal.

I found the Manover Plastics website and saw that Westnam was no longer its chief executive. I was surprised. Why hadn't Joe told me he'd left the company? His final report had been in January last year. Perhaps Westnam had left Manover after then. Where was he now?

I did a search for Roger Brookes. Again there were many references in articles to the fraud, all of which I had in my press cuttings file, including the one that told me Brookes had sold his travel agency business to Sunglow almost two years ago. I could find no other reference to him after that. Joe had provided me with his address in Gloucestershire. I would check if he was still living there and then I would pay him a visit. It was against the terms of my licence but I had to chance it. Nevertheless, I didn't want to go haring off to Gloucestershire without speaking to Joe first.

I found a call box. Joe's secretary said he wouldn't be in until Tuesday. Slightly irritated I rang directory enquiries and got the number for Manover Plastics. The lady in human resources said she had no idea where Mr Westnam was. I got the feeling that even if she did know she wouldn't have told me.

I replaced the phone, feeling tension knot my

stomach. The aeroplane incident had made me think that I needed to move quickly. Perhaps one of the business journalists who had written about Manover Plastics could tell me where its ex chief executive was, but I was reluctant to contact them. The first sniff of a story and my past could be emblazoned across the newspapers again. There was no way I wanted that.

I popped into the newsagents and bought the local weekly newspaper. Idly I scanned it and then drew up with a start. Staring at me from the front page was the name of the man I hated almost as much as Andover: DCI Clipton. What was more he was dead. I couldn't believe it. Avidly I read the small stop-press article, ignoring the fact that I was standing in the middle of the pavement and people were jostling to get around me.

### FORMER POLICE OFFICER FOUND DEAD ON WIGHT LINK FERRY

The ten o'clock Wight Link ferry, *St Catherine*, was delayed for forty minutes yesterday when a man was discovered slumped over the wheel of his car on the lower car deck.

The captain of the vessel radioed the police and a doctor pronounced the man dead before cars were allowed to disembark. The dead man is believed to have suffered a heart attack and

has been named as Michael Clipton, a retired
police superintendent of the Hampshire
Constabulary. He was fifty-eight, widowed
with a daughter.

Why had Clipton been coming to the Isle of
Wight? A holiday, perhaps? It could hardly have
been to congratulate me on my freedom.

I couldn't say that I was sorry he was dead;
rather I was annoyed and disappointed. I had
wanted to find the truth and shove it in Clipton's
face. I had dreamt of hearing his grovelling
apology and seeing the discomfort in his eyes
when he discovered he had robbed me of so
much. I felt cheated.

I telephoned the newspaper to find out where
the inquest was being held and at what time and
then I called Miles.

'Clipton's dead. He was on the ten o'clock
Wight Link ferry on Thursday.'

'Christ! The sailing before mine. They said
there was a delay. It's why I was late meeting you.
How did he die?'

'The newspaper says heart attack. I'm going to
the inquest. It's on Tuesday.'

'You think there's something suspicious about
his death?'

I heard the surprise in Miles's voice. 'I don't
know.'

I rang off with the promise that I would keep Miles informed. Three days seemed a long time to wait, especially when I was itching to get to the truth, and someone had made it clear they didn't want me to.

I collected my yacht from Ted's boatyard, where it had spent the last few years on blocks, and motored it round to moor at the end of my houseboat. I was grateful to Ted for his complete lack of curiosity about my prison life. He greeted me like an old friend and not a pariah. A ray of hope flickered inside me that others might be as forgiving as Ted. Heartened by his attitude I plucked up the courage to call Vanessa, my ex wife. There was no answer. My initial relief quickly turned to irritation, and then bitterness when there was still no answer on Saturday and Sunday. I guessed that knowing I was being released she had taken the boys away for the weekend. She probably feared that one of the first things I would do would be to attempt to see them, despite the court order banning me from having contact with them. Well, that wasn't going to stop me.

In between calls I went sailing. It was heavenly. It almost made me want to forget about Andover, Clipton and my vendetta, but not quite. Each time I returned to shore Andover was still there on my shoulder like an albatross and joining him was Clipton.

On Monday morning I collected what was left of my mother's personal belongings from her solicitor in Bembridge. William Kerry wasn't as welcoming as Ted. I got the feeling that he blamed me for my mother's death. I didn't linger long in his office. I had let Vanessa sort through my mother's possessions and decide what should be stored and kept for me on my release, and what should be discarded. I'd no option. It must have been painful for her, but not half as painful as it was for me locked in a cell unable to mourn openly, and feeling as guilty as hell over my mother's death.

I struggled out of Kerry's office with a large box and bumped right into Percy Trentham, one of my mother's oldest friends and the village gossip.

'It's Alex, isn't it?' He peered at me from underneath the peak of a grubby white baseball cap. He was pushing a lady's bicycle, complete with shopping basket, which he engineered so that it blocked my path.

I stifled a groan. 'Hello, Percy.'

'I hardly recognised you. Your hair is as white as mine. I suppose prison did that to you.'

Say it louder, why don't you? They didn't quite

hear you on the mainland.

'Heard you were out.' He pulled at his right ear and sniffed. 'Steven told me.'

How the hell did he know? Steven was Percy's son and had been my childhood friend before my mother had sent me away to a private boarding school on the mainland for which Steven had never forgiven me. I'd lost touch with him for years.

I guessed now that everyone would know about my release. I would have to steel myself to meet a certain amount of hostility. If I had wanted anonymity I shouldn't have returned here, but the houseboat and my yacht was all I had left.

Percy said, 'It can't have been easy inside for a man like you, used to the good life.' A passing couple eyed us curiously. 'Fair broke your mother's heart. I can remember her saying just before she died –'

'I can't stop.'

I hurried home with a pounding heart, cursing Percy for his thoughtless words. If this was the taste of things to come then perhaps I had better move away I thought with bitterness.

I stepped onto my houseboat and caught sight of my neighbour hanging out her washing on the deck of her houseboat. I guessed she was in her late thirties, although I could be wrong, as her clothes defied current trends, but seemed to be a mix of fashion through the decades, starting with the 1960s. Her long, multicoloured hair was blowing unchecked across her face. I certainly didn't recall her living there before I had gone to prison.

She looked up. Her gaze was unwavering. I smiled. She blanked me, picked up her washing basket and, turning her back on me, disappeared into her houseboat.

'Well sod you,' I muttered. I felt even more determined to prove to them all that I was innocent.

I steeled myself to look through what remained of my mother's possessions. She had died in the December before last, from a fall down the stairs. They had let me out for her funeral. I remembered it was a bitterly cold and grey January day. Vanessa had chosen the occasion to tell me she wanted a divorce. It still made my stomach clench every time I recalled it.

I found the official documents of the sale of Bembridge House, the deeds of the houseboat and other papers like insurances, a selection of my mother's diaries – thankfully nothing spanning the months of my arrest, trial and conviction. I didn't think I could bear to read that. There were a couple of photograph albums, and a sealed plastic bag containing some of her jewellery. It wasn't much to show for a lifetime. When Vanessa had cleared my mother's house I was beyond caring about personal possessions. I would have sold my soul for a chance of freedom.

A photograph caught my eye. It was of my mother crouching beside me, then a fair curly-haired little boy in dungarees; I was holding a small telescope to my right eye. Behind us was grandad's folly in the garden of Bembridge House. My mother was pointing at the photographer, my father, I guessed. On the back of the photograph she had written: 'Alex in the garden with his birthday present 1969.' I was four and it was March. I threw it back in the box. It reminded me too much of everything I had lost, and of my sons, David and Philip.

On Tuesday I slipped in at the back of court number four in Quay Road, Newport just as the inquest on Michael Clipton opened. There weren't many people there. A woman who I assumed to be the daughter was sitting in the front, with either her boyfriend or husband. I couldn't see her face. She was dressed in black. Behind them were a couple of men that I knew instantly to be policemen despite their not wearing uniform. On the other side of the aisle was a journalist with her notepad and beside her, in uniform, was presumably the captain of the ferry and a couple of crewmembers from the *St Catherine*. The doctor was on the stand.

I scoured the room for members of the Specialist Investigations Unit, but couldn't see anyone I knew. Neither had there been anyone following me over the last few days. There had been no dark car with tinted windows and no more incidents on my walks. And I hadn't seen the beautiful blonde again. Perhaps the aeroplane incident had just been some idiot having fun. Perhaps the blonde really had been an historian. Perhaps the car with tinted windows had been visiting Sam's fishing business.

I turned my attention to the doctor as he told the coroner's court that Michael Clipton's arteries had been so clogged his heart attack could have happened at any time. Clipton had been on medication for high blood pressure for six years, which explained his red face as he had thrust it close to mine during his interrogations.

A crewmember told how all the cars had been vacant of their passengers and drivers, as the ferry had sailed out of Portsmouth at 10am, and again half way across the Solent when he had checked. Forty minutes later, as the ferry approached Fishbourne, the passengers were told to return to their cars, which they all did. Another crewmember told how all the decks were clear of passengers as the *St Catherine* hit the big wooden fenders at Fishbourne.

Clipton, it seemed, had returned to his car, sat in it and died. It was just one of those things, or so I thought until the daughter took the stand. She was about thirty-five with short straight fair hair and a worried expression on her long, oval face. She spoke softly, and had difficulty in holding the coroner's eye contact. She said that she'd had no idea that her father was coming to the Isle of Wight. Why should she, I thought, Clipton didn't have to tell his daughter his movements, which was exactly what the coroner, a grey, shrivelled-up man, said.

'He *would* have told me,' the daughter declared, flushing. 'I would have worried about him otherwise. Since Mum died and Dad retired he's always kept me informed if he was going to be away from the house longer than a couple of days.'

'And this time he didn't tell you?'

'Oh yes, he did.'

The coroner looked confused and a little exasperated. I didn't blame him. She must have seen his irritation because she blushed and added, 'I knew he *was* going away but I didn't know he was coming to the Isle of Wight. I thought he was going to Andover.'

What? Had I heard right? I sat bolt upright as if someone had shoved an electric poker up my backside.

'Andover?' The coroner sounded like Lady Bracknell and her handbag. I guessed that Andover wasn't the sort of place you went on holiday to.

'Did he have business in Andover?'

'Business? He's retired.' She looked confused. Her eyes welled up. 'He *was* retired.' A sob caught in her throat.

I couldn't imagine anyone mourning the bastard who had interrogated and bullied me, but then I was prejudiced.

'Yes, of course,' the coroner said, hastily and a little irritably. He didn't seem to me the best candidate for this job. I wondered if he had been the coroner at my mother's inquest. I shuddered at the vision of my poor mother's death being scrutinized like this. Yet it had been and without me being present. The verdict had been accidental death. I couldn't have prevented it even if I had been free. It was small consolation. Hastily I pulled myself together and focused on what the coroner was saying.

'So he told you he was going to Andover for a couple of days' holiday.'

'No. He just said, 'I'll be away for a couple of days, possibly a few; I'm not sure. I'm going to Andover,' Clipton's daughter replied.

My eyes swept the room. I held my breath, waiting for someone to stand up and say, Andover's a man not a town in Hampshire. No one did. The police didn't even look interested. I swivelled in my seat to look behind me, there was no one either sitting or standing. The doors were shut. I needed to speak to Clipton's daughter, but away from here and in private, without two policemen breathing down my neck, wondering who the hell I was, putting two and two together and coming up with eight.

A verdict was brought in of death by natural causes. The coroner gave permission for the body to be released and I slipped out before anyone else into a day that threatened April showers. I watched from the safety of the opposite side of the road as they spilled out of the inquest. I saw the two policemen move forward and fall into conversation with Clipton's daughter and partner, who was a slightly overweight man with a little goatee beard that was beginning to turn grey. Their heads were nodding, their expressions serious. Then they all climbed into a car and were driven off. I cursed. I guessed they were leaving the Island.

A payphone was just a few yards to my left and I dived into it and rang Miles's office. After a brief moment I was put through to him.

'Clipton's daughter said he was going to Andover.'

'And you think that means he was coming to see you?'

Clipton had always believed that I was Andover. 'Either that or Andover is or was on the Island.' And that might explain the aeroplane incident. It didn't explain, though, why he hadn't tried to attack me again. 'The only person who might know more is his daughter. I'm going to Clipton's funeral. There I can ask her a couple of questions under the guise of passing on my condolences. She won't know who I am.'

'Unless someone tells her.'

'I'll take a chance on that. Besides they might not recognise me now.'

I heard Miles sniff in disbelief. 'Perhaps I should go instead.'

'Miles, I'm a big boy. I can take care of myself.' Then sensing I'd spoken too harshly, I added, 'Thanks, but this is my battle. I'm grateful for everything you've done and how you've stuck with me but I have to stand on my own two feet. There is something you *can* do for me though.'

'You've got it.'

'Find out when and where Clipton's funeral is. Perhaps one of your contacts in the police can tell you. I'll call you tomorrow.'

I rang off and called Joe. His secretary told me I had just missed him. He was on an assignment and wouldn't be back until Friday. She wouldn't give me his mobile number either. I was beginning to get the feeling he was avoiding me. I said I would call again on Friday.

It had started raining but judging by the speed of the clouds a blue bit of sky was due at any moment so I ducked into the café in the Quay Arts Centre, and fetched myself a coffee. I couldn't help feeling a thrill of excitement. OK, so Clipton's death had been due to natural causes, but why had he been coming here? And why tell his daughter he was going to Andover? If Andover had been on the Island then it was bloody convenient for him that Clipton had died.

I was impatient for an appointment to see Joe, and for Clipton's funeral. Perhaps then, at last, I'd start getting some answers.

## Chapter 3

The following Monday morning I alighted from the hovercraft at Portsmouth. It was a grey, gloomy day with a chill edge to the breeze and the threat of rain in the air. The right sort of day for a burial, I thought, as I skirted Southsea Common and headed towards the city centre. Clipton's committal was at one o'clock. That gave me plenty of time for my meeting with Joe, which I'd finally managed to arrange on Friday.

I spotted the fair-haired man with the square jaw and stooping posture as I waited to cross Kings Road. He had been on the hovercraft.

Nothing odd in that, lots of people travel to Portsmouth, but I felt uneasy. I smelt a copper.

I zipped up my sailing jacket, turned right into Landport Street and right again, or rather I would have done, if the road hadn't been blocked by blue and white police tape, a stout copper and a small crowd. My heart skipped a beat. Almost instantly I knew why they were here. Suddenly the energy and optimism drained from me. It had to be Joe. If it was then there was only one reason why something should have happened to him now: me.

I craned my neck to see a police car straddling the road of terraced houses, small offices and council flats, its blue light pulsating. My flesh crawled. I glanced nervously behind me but the fair-haired man was nowhere in sight. I watched the white-suited scene of crime team come and go. A television cameraman and reporter were further along to my right.

'What's happened?' I asked a black man next to me.

'Man been attacked,' he said.

'Is he all right?'

'If he is, he ain't breathing none too well with the body-bag zipped up over his face. I seen it come out half an hour ago.'

'Who is it?'

'Dunno.' He shrugged his broad shoulders, but the woman next to him said:

'I heard one of the policemen say it was a private detective and that he must have been working on a pretty nasty divorce case to get himself killed.'

God! Where would this end? Would it *ever* end?

I hung around a bit longer but couldn't pick up any further bits of gossip. Disappointed and worried I ducked into the nearest café, which was full of students. Nursing my coffee in as dark a corner as I could find I wondered what to do. If I came forward and told the police that I'd had an appointment with Joe they'd ask me why. Before I knew it I'd be in a police station answering questions, or, as they so euphemistically put it, helping with their enquiries, until they could eliminate me. I was out on licence. One sniff of trouble and they'd have me back inside before you could say porridge. The memory was enough to bring me out in a cold sweat and turn the contents of my stomach to liquid. But what if Joe had entered our appointment in a diary? Did he keep a diary? Did his secretary?

'You all right, dear? You looks a bit queasy to me.'

I glanced up to see a middle-aged waitress with blonde frizzled hair, tight cheap clothes, excessive make-up and a worried frown on her lined face. She was wiping down the table next to me. She didn't seem to fit with the café, which was full of youthful vigour, clear skins and trouble-free expressions. Still she wasn't the only one: I hardly blended!

She said, 'I expect it's the murder round the corner; fair turns you over, don't it. You're not safe these days. I've heard it's poor Mr Bristow. Such a nice man, never did no one no harm. Used to come in here regular like for a coffee and a doughnut, or a nice fry-up for breakfast. Hard to believe.'

She smiled sadly before strutting off on heels that were ridiculously high and thin. Not for me it wasn't hard to believe. Things happened to me and around me. Had my call to Joe warned Andover that I was on his trail? How could Andover have known that unless Joe's phone was tapped? It seemed incredulous but then as Andover had managed to manipulate my computer files, a simple case of phone tapping certainly wouldn't be beyond him. Besides, I'd learnt in prison that you could easily buy electronic listening devices on the Internet or by mail order.

I considered another possibility that had occurred to me more than once over the last few years. Could Andover be an electronics or computer expert? I didn't know anyone like that. At least I didn't think I did. It could be someone I had been at school or university with, who might have entered one of those fields. If so it had to be someone who hated me because I had hurt him in some way. I couldn't think of anyone who fitted the picture, except Steven Trentham, but that was impossible.

I turned my mind back to poor Joe. Why kill him? The obvious answer was because Andover was scared that Joe might tell me something. Which meant there was something to tell. Then why hadn't Joe already told it to me? Perhaps he had but its importance had eluded me. Time for me to go over the reports he had sent me, yet again.

I sat up. The reports! Shit! I hoped they were OK where I had left them on the houseboat. I almost hurried home then, but soon realised there was little point. If Andover was after them, they'd be long gone by the time I returned home.

Whichever way I looked at it someone had known I was coming here, and that someone had made sure that Joe wasn't going to be alive when I arrived. Then a thought struck me, if Andover had listened in to Joe's telephone calls, perhaps the police had too. Perhaps they had bargained on my coming to see Joe on my release, which meant they could already be looking for me.

I sipped my coffee racking my brains trying to recall how that conversation had run:

'Joe, it's Alex Albury. Do you remember me?'

'Of course I do, Mr Albury. How are you doing?'

'I'm out on parole. I'd like to come and see you.'

'I've got nothing for you, Mr Albury. The trail was as cold as a freezer in Iceland.'

'Maybe, but I'd still like to talk to you. I'd like to go over what you did, who you spoke to, what you found.'

'I found nothing.'

'Would Monday suit you, about eleven? I'll pay for your time.'

'OK, if it'll make you happy. But don't build your hopes up.'

If the police *had* bugged Joe's calls, then I'd know soon enough.

I finished my coffee, paid my bill and headed out. I was early for Clipton's funeral but I didn't mind. It would take me a while to walk across the city to the cemetery where Miles had told me Clipton was being buried. I checked to see if I was being followed but the fair-haired man had gone.

By the time I reached the vast cemetery on the eastern side of Portsmouth the dark clouds were gathering overhead and the wind was snatching at the trees scattering the blossom from them like confetti at a wedding. I sat amongst the flaking and lichen-covered tombstones listening to the birds chirping and watching the squirrels' antics. My mother had been cremated. I was glad. I didn't like to think of her flesh and bones rotting away inside the earth.

I shuddered and lifted my collar as the first spots of rain fell. With Joe dead my hopes rested on Clipton's daughter giving me some answers to my questions. As if on cue cars began to pull into the cemetery. I glimpsed her black-clothed figure in the limousine behind the hearse. I followed the cars to Clipton's grave and then ducked behind a large memorial angel, weathered in white marble, and made out like I was a mourner.

Either Clipton had a big family or he had been well liked, and this made me wonder if Joe had any family, perhaps a wife he had confided in. I knew he didn't have a partner but what about his secretary? She must have typed up his reports. Perhaps she could tell me something. Or was she in danger herself? I sincerely hoped not, but I wasn't betting on it.

I scanned the crowd. The police officers weren't hard to spot as experience and my cellmates had taught me how. There was no one I recognised. Not even Clipton's softly spoken sergeant who had played nice guy to Clipton's mean and angry one. I wondered what had happened to him. Even if he'd been transferred surely he would have been here. Perhaps they hadn't got on.

The cemetery seemed deserted save for us. It was raining now quite heavily and the curate was having a job holding the umbrella over the vicar in the tempestuous wind.

My only chance of speaking to the daughter would be after the committal when the other mourners made their way back to their cars. Then, on the pretence of giving my condolences, I could ask her what her father had said about Andover. Either that or I would have to follow them back to the house, but that would be risky given the police presence, as someone might recognise me. I hadn't really thought of how I was going to broach the subject but knew that something would come to me. I hadn't been a PR man for over thirteen years for nothing.

The committal seemed to go on forever. The wind strengthened and with it came heavier rain; it was mean, slanting stuff that stung my face and seeped through my trousers and shoes. Clipton, it appeared, was having the last laugh on us. The only good thing about it, I thought, was that the mourners would be in a hurry to leave. And they were. His daughter remained; along with the man I'd seen her with at the inquest. Holding his hand, and clutching a handkerchief, she stared down at the coffin as the vicar snatched a surreptitious and anxious glance at his watch.

Now was my chance and I was going to take it. I had to repeat myself before I penetrated her sorrow.

'I'm sorry about your father.' I wasn't, but I had to observe the niceties.

She twitched her lips in the ghost of a smile that never touched her eyes. Her partner smiled encouragingly at her.

'Are you ready, Christine?' he asked gently.

She nodded and the three of us began to move off. The vicar and curate followed. Ahead of us, huddled by the cars, were the other mourners, faces screwed up against the harshness of the weather. My face was so wet that the rain ran off it in rivulets. My trousers were clinging to my legs like melted plastic. But what was a bit of rain to me? I'd known worse.

I was wondering how to broach the subject

when she became conscious that I was beside her.

'Did you work with my father?' she said, her voice seeming to come from a great distance away.

Poor cow, she looked so bedraggled and forlorn, her fair hair was dark with the rain and plastered to her head. Her eyes held such pain and sorrow that told me she must have loved him. I tried to imagine Clipton as a loving father, but couldn't.

'No. But I knew him through his work.' It seemed to satisfy her. Her partner was too concerned about her to detect any double meaning or sinister intent.

'I can't think what he was doing on the Isle of Wight,' she suddenly burst out. I could see it was a question that had been vexing her ever since she had heard the news of his death.

For a spilt second I tossed up what to say and decided that half the truth might get me somewhere – where, I didn't know, and only time and daring would tell. 'I think he might have been coming to see me.'

That brought her up sharply. She stopped to stare at me whilst over her shoulder I could see the other mourners getting impatient and beginning to clamber into their cars.

'Why?'

Before I could answer the husband spoke. 'You didn't say at the inquest?'

He'd noticed me there then. 'No.'

'Why was he coming to see you?' she repeated, a dazed expression on her face.

'Because of Andover.'

'But… I thought... what do you mean?'

'Come on, honey, let's get out of the rain, the other mourners are waiting.'

'No.' She shook him off and turned a penetrating gaze upon me as though I had suddenly woken her from sleepwalking. 'What do you mean?'

Time to be economical with the truth. 'Your father and I met four years ago in the course of his work. I can't tell you much about it, you understand.' She nodded enthusiastically. I had made it sound as if we were both working on counter-espionage. 'We were looking for someone called Andover. We didn't find him. I live on the Isle of Wight. Your father could have been coming to tell me he had found Andover.'

'I don't know. It doesn't…'

'Please, honey, you're soaked.'

I scowled at him. 'Can you recall exactly what your father said?'

Her brow furrowed in thought. 'All I can remember is that he said, I must go to Andover.

No, hold on, he said, I'm going to *see* Andover.'

'He said "see"?'

'Yes, I remember now because I thought it was an odd expression. You might go and see Naples but you don't usually say I must go and *see* Andover.'

'Did he leave any notes, memoirs, records, a diary?'

'No. The police asked me that. His colleagues…' I saw her glance go beyond me and knew that they were there. They had been watching me, and waiting.

'Was your father carrying a briefcase or notebook when he died?'

'No. He had a small bag with him containing some of his clothes.'

'What about his mobile phone?'

'I…'

'Christine, please,' her partner urged, glaring at me.

'One more thing. Do you know where I can find Sergeant Hammond? He used to work with your father,' I explained when she looked at me a little blankly.

Her face brightened. 'He lives in Spain. He retired before Dad.'

'Wasn't he too young to retire?' I asked surprised.

'He won the lottery, or premium bonds, I think.'

Her husband took her arm firmly. 'Come on.' This time she didn't protest. But before she had gone a couple of paces she turned back.

'If you find out what Dad was doing, will you come and tell me?'

I nodded. 'Where do you live?'

'Give him one of your business cards, Mark.'

With a heavy sigh, Mark struggled for his pocket under his large dark-blue anorak and retrieved a tattered card, which he handed to me. I saw from it that he was a graphic designer.

'If you remember anything else, or find anything that you think might be helpful, will you call me?' It was my turn to scrabble for a piece of paper, which I found but I didn't have a telephone so I wrote down Miles's mobile number. 'You can contact me through this. He'll pass any message on to me.'

She took it, thrust it in her pocket and headed for the car. I watched her climb into the sleek, black limousine and drive off. Then a fist gripped my shoulder. I stiffened before turning. I knew who it would be. The police.

# CHAPTER 4

'I think it's time we had a chat, Alex. Detective Chief Inspector Crowder.'

I would like to have refused but, judging by the man's expression, I didn't think I had much choice.

'Shall we get out of this rain?' Crowder said.

His voice was surprisingly quiet for one so large. It was well cultured and caressing too, but it didn't fool me. Underneath I knew was a hard bastard. He was wearing a Homburg and a huge macintosh that reached almost to his ankles; all he needed was a gun slung over his arm and a pair of Hunters to look as if he was out on a country shoot. Beside him was a thin man with a short rain jacket that barely covered his narrow backside; he had soaking wet trousers, and a rather bored expression on his lean face.

'I'm wet already so it doesn't make any difference,' I said, hunching my shoulders and ramming my hands into the pockets of my jacket.

'It does to me, Alex. Perhaps we can give you a lift somewhere.' It wasn't a question. A face like his was made to command.

'The Isle of Wight?' I ventured.

Crowder's smile didn't touch his eyes. 'I was thinking more in the way of the hovercraft.'

It didn't surprise me that he knew where I had come from. It wouldn't have surprised me if he knew what I'd eaten for breakfast. Men like him knew everything.

We walked towards his car in silence. The man with the narrow backside opened the rear door and I climbed in. There was little else I could do; besides it would save me the bus fare.

'That is Sergeant Adams.' Crowder pointed at the neck of the skinny man now in the driver's seat. Adams' eyes flicked to the rear view mirror and connected with mine. I raised my eyebrows in a kind of acknowledgement but got nothing in return. I hadn't really expected it.

Crowder removed his hat, revealing a luxuriant head of silver hair, which was swept back off his broad forehead. I stared at his taciturn face and cold assessing eyes and felt my stomach churn. I knew he would be an even more formidable adversary than Clipton.

Crowder said, 'You went to see Joe Bristow, why?'

'You know why.' That brought a smile of sorts to his lips.

'I've been told you're clever.'

'Don't think much of your informant then. I wasn't clever enough to avoid DCI Clipton and prison,' I replied acerbically.

Silence for a few moments as the car stopped and started its way back towards the seafront. Every now and again I caught the sergeant's glance in the rear-view mirror. I marvelled at his ability to look so disinterested. I could have done with some tips from him during my first year in prison.

'What were you doing at Chief Inspector Clipton's funeral?' Crowder's voice broke through my unhappy memories. I was rather glad.

'I went to make sure the bastard really was dead,' I snapped. Before prison I wouldn't have dreamed of speaking to a police officer so dismissively or sarcastically. I had been brought up to respect the law. Now everything was different, including me. I tried not to show my tension. I knew Crowder would see it and perceive it as a weakness. Ray's words came to me. '*Show the bastards you don't give a toss. That way they can't hurt you, even when they do hurt you*'.

Crowder shook his big head like a St Bernard dog, and a sorrowful expression swept across his lugubrious face. 'You're not *still* trying to prove that you're innocent, are you, Alex? I don't think the parole board will take a good view of that. Didn't you tell them how sorry you are and that you'd hand the money over *if* you could lay your hands on it?'

Of course Crowder would know what the parole board report had said. 'Is that what you're after? Well, I'm sorry to disappoint. I haven't a clue where it is.'

'No? We've long since come to the conclusion that Andover doesn't exist. He was your alter ego. You were and are Andover.'

*I* knew I wasn't. 'Traffic's heavy.' *Say nothing. Show nothing* – Ray again.

'Why was Clipton travelling to the Isle of Wight? Did you arrange to meet him?' Crowder said, with a harder edge to his voice.

'Hardly. Perhaps he fancied a holiday.'

'Where's the three million pounds you stole, Alex?'

'It's stopped raining.'

'All right, let's try another one. Where were you between nine and eleven this morning?'

I swivelled to look directly at him. 'You know where I was. I was making my way from my houseboat to Ryde to catch the hovercraft. And if you ask your fair-haired detective he will verify that I was nowhere near Joe Bristow's office until just before eleven.'

Crowder smiled which made me more uncomfortable than before. I had struck lucky with the fair-haired detective theory, but I felt uneasy. Why had he been so obvious? I had the feeling that I was intended to spot him.

The sergeant pulled up outside the hovercraft terminal. Before I could climb out Crowder said in that deceptively comforting voice, 'You've got that money, Alex, and I'm going to find out where it is. OK, so you may not have killed Joe Bristow yourself, but you know who did. You may even have ordered his death.' He held up his hand to prevent me from protesting. I couldn't anyway; I was struck dumb by what he was saying. My mouth must have been agape with amazement. He continued, 'I'll get you in the end, Alex. I just thought you ought to know that.'

As I watched the car drive off I felt cold with fear. Crowder's threats weren't empty ones.

There was also something personal in the way he had spoken. My God, as if I hadn't been through a bad enough time with DCI Clipton, now I had another vindictive copper on my back. My fear swiftly turned to anger. It fed my determination to find Andover and clear my name. I'd take great pleasure in ramming that down the smug bastard's throat.

I waited until the car was out of sight, then turned westwards towards Old Portsmouth and the High Street, where Miles's office was based. My mind wandered back to my conversation with Clipton's daughter, which I'd hardly had time to digest with Crowder breathing down my neck. Why had Clipton taken an overnight bag with him to the Island? Who had he arranged to see? Had he booked in anywhere? Where was his mobile phone? I couldn't recall them mentioning it at the coroner's inquest. Clipton must have had one and it would show who he had called. I was heartily glad the houseboat didn't have a telephone and that I didn't have a mobile. If Clipton had called Camp Hill Prison to enquire after me then the screws hadn't told me. And where were his notebooks? All police officers carried notebooks and nearly all ex-police officers kept their old ones when they retired. DCI Crowder knew a hell of a lot more than he was saying.

A young woman with heavy perfume and pubescent hips showed me up to Miles's office on the first floor. I got the impression that she found me rather attractive. I'd heard from some of my fellow inmates that they had no trouble finding women when they came out. I guessed ex-cons were a challenge to them, a man with a hint of danger and mystery, someone to reform. For a moment I wondered what had happened to the blonde bombshell I'd met in Brading church.

'I'm up to my armpits with work.' Miles waved me into seat across the black ash desk piled with papers. He looked as though he hadn't slept in days. His tie was askew, his sleeves rolled up showing his strong hairy forearms. There were dark circles under his bloodshot eyes and a more than usual haggard expression on his craggy face. 'I've got a big court case coming up, and I've got to prepare the papers for the barrister. Man accused of food contamination and he doesn't much care if he goes down for it. Claims it will be a blow for consumers against capitalism.'

'Tell him he's wasting his breath. I doubt it'll dent the supermarkets' profits and no one gives a flying fart about principles in prison,' I said caustically.

'I'll pass your message on,' Miles said, with the

twist of a smile. He picked up a pencil and began tapping it on the desk.

I said, 'Joe's dead.'

That brought him up sharp. 'What? When? You're kidding!'

'Afraid not. His street is crawling with police.'

'Bloody hell! How?'

'For some reason the police didn't seem to want to take me into their confidence.'

'The police have interviewed you!' He looked shocked.

'A DCI Crowder and Sergeant Adams gave me a lift back from Clipton's funeral. They wanted to know where I was between nine and eleven this morning, presumably when Joe was killed. It's rather a coincidence that Joe was killed on the morning I was due to visit him, don't you think? Which means that Joe must have known something about Andover and was going to tell me. It also means that Andover knew I was going to see Joe.'

I told him my theory about Joe's phone possibly being tapped. He didn't look at me as if I'd gone mad. Miles had too much experience of the criminal fraternity for that.

'Apart from the obvious, who else knows I'm out?'

'Vanessa does. I called her to tell her.'

'Which means her new husband knows.'

'Yes. Gus Newberry.'

I wondered what he was like? How did he compare with me? What did my sons think of him? I felt myself tense at the thought of Gus Newberry doing all the things with my boys that I had once done, like kicking a football, teasing them, putting them to bed…Roughly I pushed such thoughts away. 'There's also Joe's secretary,' I growled.

'Joy! I can't see her involved in this.'

'I don't know her, but I'd like to talk to her.'

'I can arrange that. There is another alternative…'

'Joe contacted Andover and told him I was coming to see him. Yes, I had considered that. Maybe Joe thought Andover would kill me, but silenced Joe instead.'

'Which means –'

'That Joe found out who Andover was and did some kind of deal with him. That's why he told me the trail was cold. It's why he never found out why Westnam, Couldner and Brookes allowed themselves to be blackmailed. Yes, it had crossed my mind.'

Miles let out a long slow breath. 'Where does DCI Crowder fit in?'

'I'm not sure, except he thinks I killed Joe, or was an accomplice to his death. I assumed he was from specialist investigations. He knew all about me.'

'I'll find out. Joe was handling a couple of cases for me. I'll talk to Detective Superintendent Reede; he's head of the Major Crime Team. I expect he'll send someone to interview me.'

'What will you say if they ask you about me?' I asked a little anxiously.

'I'll tell them the truth - *if* they ask me the right questions.' He smiled. 'But they might not know what the right questions are.'

'Miles, don't get into trouble.'

He cut me short with a smile. 'You're forgetting I'm a criminal lawyer and a good one at that, with one exception: you.'

Yes.

'Was Joe married?'

'Divorced. How did you get on at the funeral?'

'Jennifer Clipton told me that Sergeant Hammond, Clipton's second in command, won the lottery or the pools or something, chucked in his job and took off for sunny Spain. Can you check it out for me?'

'You think he might have been paid off?'

I shrugged. 'If Andover bought Joe off, he might have bought Hammond too. And see what you can find out about DCI Clipton's death. I know the coroner said natural causes, and it probably was, but see if the police are satisfied with that.'

'How do I get in touch with you?'

'I'll ring you. I've given Jennifer Clipton your telephone number; she'll call you if she remembers anything that can throw a light on what her father was doing visiting the Isle of Wight. Could you ask Joe's secretary if she'll meet me?'

'Of course. Where?'

'Wherever she wants.'

I glanced at my watch. It was almost four o'clock. 'Could you try her now?'

Miles picked up his phone. 'She won't be in the office. I'll try her mobile.'

I crossed to the window as he called her number.

'Joy, it's Miles.'

His voice faded into the distance as I stared at the grey brick façade of the grammar school opposite. It was where Vanessa had once taught, and where our boys had gone to school. Vanessa had suggested I try Miles's law firm. After my trial and conviction Vanessa had resigned her job as assistant head teacher. She'd since found a new job teaching at a private school just outside Petersfield, which the boys now attended. It was close to where they lived with their stepfather.

My eyes travelled along the road to where a stocky man wearing a crash helmet was standing beside his motorbike, looking this way. Was he following me? Was he a copper?

I wondered if Joy would tell me anything. Would she still have those reports that Joe had compiled on his investigation into Andover? Had she handed them over to the police? Or had Joe destroyed them? Perhaps Andover had done that after killing Joe. If they were the same reports I had then I knew they weren't worth the paper they were written on. But what if Joe had sent me edited highlights and the real reports contained some clue as to the identity and whereabouts of Andover? I had to check.

Miles came off the phone. 'Ten o'clock tomorrow.'

Damn. I had hoped it would be today. I said, 'Where?'

'The café in the Portsmouth Museum.'

That seemed as good a place as any.

The day was drawing in earlier than usual because of the now relentless rain and heavy skies and I was surprised to find my neighbour waiting for me in the small forecourt of my houseboat when I returned home. Her long, very wet hair in various shades of brown was framing a

scowling face. She wore a long flowing green
raincoat that reached Doc Martin-type boots.

'Have you seen my mother?' She demanded
before I had even pushed back the gate. She was
glaring at me as if I'd kidnapped her.

I didn't even know she had a mother. 'No. I've
just returned from the mainland.'

She looked cross, as if it had been irresponsible
of me to leave when her mother had gone missing.

'She might be inside your houseboat.'

'I doubt it. It's locked.' I could see that she
wasn't going to believe me, so I opened up and
we stepped inside. 'What's her name?'

'Ruby Kingston.'

'And yours?'

I could see she was reluctant to tell me. I
thought she was going to tell me to mind my
own business, but after a moment she said,
'Scarlett and no cracks about *Gone with the Wind*.'

'It's a very pretty name. Mine's Alex Albury,
but I expect you know that already.'

She sniffed and scoured the interior of my
lounge as if her mother could have been secreted
somewhere.

'I wasn't convicted of kidnap or murder,' I
snapped, irritated by her manner.

'Makes no difference to me what you went
down for.'

'Or that I was innocent?'

She gave a cynical smile. 'That's what they all say.'

'In my case it happens to be true. What made you think she could be here?'

'She forgets where she lives. She knocks on all the houseboats along here and I thought she might have got in without you realising it.'

I was about to say that I thought I would have noticed an old lady rattling around the place when something in her expression prevented me. Behind her scowling countenance I could see genuine concern in her large brown eyes.

'I'm sure she'll turn up,' I said gently, but she mistook my meaning.

'Oh yes, she'll turn up, perhaps dead on the beach, washed up by the tide. She might even turn up in the mortuary after being knocked down by a car.'

'Look, I –'

'Forget it. What do you care anyway?'

She stormed out and I was left feeling shocked by her sudden outburst and then angry with her. I dismissed her and her mother from my mind, made myself something to eat and took the folder of Joe's reports from underneath the mattress where I had stowed it. A bloody silly place, I know, and the first place Andover would have looked. I read through them again. There didn't seem to be anything in them that Andover would be interested in.

Roger Brookes' house was just outside a village called Wootton-under-Edge in Gloucestershire; Joe had furnished me with the address two years ago. That must have been just before Brookes had sold out to Sunglow. I jotted the details down in my notebook and lay back on the bed. The couple of whiskies I'd drunk had made me sleepy.

I was woken by a noise. I glanced at my watch and was surprised to see that it was almost ten o'clock. The noise came again; someone was trying to get in. Suddenly I was alert. I stuffed my notebook into the pocket of my trousers and crept to the door. I threw it open to find a very wet and very distressed old lady on my doorstep. This must be Ruby.

'Hugo!' she cried, tumbling into my arms and pressing her soaking wet head against my chest, her body heaving with sobs; I could see her pink scalp through her wispy grey hair. Her dress was sodden and her legs and feet filthy. Disgust was my first reaction, followed swiftly by fear, not of her but of my reaction: I had wanted to push her away. I folded my arms around her frail body. It seemed to give her some comfort because the sobs eased. I wondered who Hugo was?

'You're safe now. Come on, sit down.' I eased her towards the bench and prised her arms from around my back lowering her onto the seat. 'Have you got a handkerchief in your bag?'

Her head came up and she stared at me alarmed. Clutching her handbag tight to her waist she wailed, 'Don't you come near me. I know what you're after.'

I descended to the kitchen to fetch a towel and some tissues. By the time I returned she'd gone and the door was flapping open in the wind. I cursed loudly and vehemently, pulled on my sailing jacket, grabbed a torch and stepped out into the wild April night.

She was a few hundred yards down, stumbling towards Bembridge village. I needed to go after her and bring her back, but she might think I was attacking her, and before I knew it the police would be swarming all over me.

I bounded up to my neighbour's houseboat and beat on the door. There was no answer. Of course, she'd be out looking for her mother.

Ruby had reached the café that led down onto the beach. If she stumbled onto the shore she might very well end up in the sea, as her daughter had predicted. There was nothing for it but to go after her.

I saw her turn right though, away from the shore and onto the track in front of the Pilot Boat Inn. She disappeared from sight. I sprinted after her, knowing that the path would take her past the backs of houses that overlooked the harbour, through the trees and eventually up to the windmill. It would be dark, muddy and dangerous.

A shaft of light sliced across me as the door of the pub opened and with it came the sound of laughter before it shut again. A man stared at me. There was something familiar about him. I couldn't place what, and I didn't have time to ask him.

I caught up with Ruby after another five hundred yards. I almost ran into her. She was staring up at the back of a large house part shaded by the trees. It was in darkness but its sweeping lawns led down to a folly and its rear windows looked out across Bembridge Harbour and across to Portsmouth, beyond the Solent. I knew this because it had been my home, and my mother's before her death three years ago. That lump the size of a golf ball was back in my throat. A pain gripped my heart and my breath came in painful gasps as I struggled to control my overwhelming sorrow. I should have been with her when she died. I should have been able to say good-bye. Andover would pay for that.

I took a deep breath and pushed aside my emotions with some difficulty. Why had Ruby come here?

I stood silently beside her, as if she was an animal I didn't want to scare off. She was obliviously to the elements that buffeted her. After a moment she spoke with an edge of bewilderment to her voice.

'He used to stay here.'

'Who did?'

'Hugo. He was so lovely. Where has he gone? What have you done with him?' She turned her anguished face to mine. It was smeared with pink lipstick and her thick face powder had run making it look like dirty rain on a windowpane. Her skin was spongy and criss-crossed with lines, and her milky blue eyes sad.

So she no longer thought I was Hugo. 'Come on, Ruby, let's get you home,' I said. I didn't dare touch her. How could I get her away from here? She was shivering and soaked.

'He pushed her down the stairs.'

That pulled me up with a start. My heart did a somersault. 'Do you mean Olivia Albury?'

'Yes. She was my friend.'

So that's why she had come here. But she was mistaken. 'No one killed Olivia. She fell. It was an accident.' At least that was what the police and the coroner had said. A sliver of fear ran through me.

Ruby peered at me. 'I *saw* him push her.'

She was very insistent. Could she be telling the truth? But why would anyone want to kill my mother? Then again, why would anyone want to frame me? But they had.

The charity that Andover had set up had been registered at this address, and even though there had been a re-direct on the mail perhaps an item of post had got through. Had my mother discovered the identity of Andover and that's why she had been killed? The thought startled me so much that I found myself trembling. Not without effort I pulled myself together and brought my attention back to the old lady beside me.

'Come on, Ruby. Let's get you home.' How could I believe what she was saying? She was old and confused. She stepped back. Her eyes widened. I could see that at any moment she would scream.

'You're going to kill me too.'

'No one's going to hurt you, Ruby.'

She looked doubtful. I made a decision. I turned my back on her and began walking away hoping that she would follow. After a few moments I heard soft, hurrying footsteps behind me. I didn't dare turn round in case she scuttled off again. We reached the Embankment. I was just debating what to do short of locking her on my houseboat when I saw a figure hurrying towards me. Thank goodness, it was Scarlett.

'Mum, I've been searching everywhere for you.' She took her mother's arm and gently led her forward to their houseboat.

'She was at the back of Bembridge House. It's where I used to live.'

'I know.'

'She says my mother was pushed down the stairs. Is there any truth in that?'

'She's got Alzheimer's.'

Ruby suddenly piped up. 'I hid in Teddy's room. I thought he might do the same to me, only he didn't come back.'

My heart quickened. Teddy had been my grandfather. Ruby had got the geography of Bembridge House correct but my grandfather had been dead for sixty-seven years.

'Do you know anyone called Hugo?' I addressed Scarlett.

'No.'

'What did he look like, Ruby?'

'I don't remember.'

'I need to get Mum to bed.'

And that was it. It was clear Scarlett didn't

approve of me. Well that was her problem not mine. I had enough on my mind without worrying about an old lady with dementia and a hostile daughter.

I told myself that Ruby's picture of the past had become confused with the present. Yet, as I made my way to Portsmouth the next morning to keep my appointment with Joe's secretary, I knew I was kidding myself. If I had needed another reason to destroy Andover this was it. If Andover had killed my mother then I was going to make him suffer for it.

## CHAPTER 5

Joy Hardiman wasn't what I had expected. She was tall as me and I'm six one in my stocking feet. She wore two-inch heels. I wore loafers. Her handshake was perfunctory but firm. She was older than I had expected, in her late forties, with cropped auburn hair, freckles on a small round face and lively green eyes. I hadn't expected anyone so elegantly dressed either, in smart tailored chocolate-brown trousers, and an oatmeal polo neck jumper, under a brown leather jacket. But then Joe hadn't exactly been what you might call your typical private eye, all shabby suits, dandruff and scruffy hair. Instead he had sported a crewcut of greying hair and had always been very neatly turned out in a well tailored suit and tie, or at least he had when he'd visited me in prison. This was twice, before I'd been moved from Brixton to the Isle of Wight.

'Coffee?'

'I've got one,' she said.

'I'll just fetch myself one then.'

I scanned the small café on the ground floor. A group of four young people, two girls and two boys, sat hunched over their mobile phones; a scruffy-looking middle-aged man, the frayed ends of his trousers hanging over his scuffed shoes, was reading the *Independent*; a large man, the colour of coal, wearing sunglasses that were too small for his bullet-shaped head, was listening to music on his headphones, and two women in colourful saris were chattering nineteen to the dozen, whilst their four children played at their feet. Then there was Joy who didn't live up to her name as she stared down into her coffee cup.

'It's good of you to meet me.' I placed my coffee on the table and took the seat opposite her.

'Miles said it was important. That it might have something to do with Joe's … death.'

'I'm sorry about Joe,' I said gently. 'You must be very upset.'

She took a deep breath. 'I shall miss him.' She spoke with a slight lisp but her voice though sad was steady and I recognised a sensible woman when I saw one.

'Was Joe working on something connected to me?'

'The police asked me that.'

I felt a tightening in my gut but was confident that my expression hadn't betrayed my tension. Prison had taught me how to hide or disguise emotion. 'A well built man with a Homburg and huge macintosh?'

'Yes.'

'When?'

'Yesterday morning.'

So the fat man was on to me even before I arrived at Clipton's funeral. 'What did you tell him?'

'The same as I'm going to tell you: Joe dropped your case ages ago.'

A couple of women entered laughing. Joy glared at them as if they had personally insulted her. I knew what she was thinking: how could they be so happy when she felt so miserable over the death of her boss?

'Why did he drop my case?'

'He said he would never be able to find Andover unless he decided to return to England.'

'Joe knew he'd left the country?' I asked, surprised.

'He must have done. He said case closed, dead end.'

After a moment I said, 'Did Joe believe I was innocent?'

'Oh yes.'

'And you?'

'If Joe said you were then you are. His word is… was good enough for me.'

Had Joe *known* I was innocent and that was why he had convinced Joy?

'Joy, do you know where Clive Westnam lives or works?'

She looked puzzled for a moment until I jogged her mind about who he was.

Her expression cleared. 'No. The last I heard he'd been ousted from his position as chief executive of Manover Plastics. It was in the newspapers but I can't recall reading anything about where he went from there.'

'Do you know why he got the elbow?'

'Perhaps the results weren't good enough for the shareholders.'

'What about Roger Brookes? Does he still live in Gloucestershire?'

'Haven't you heard? He's dead.'

'Dead!' That shook me. It also made my heart

sink with the thought that another of Andover's victims had taken the secret of why he was being blackmailed to his grave. That only left Westnam, and for all I knew, and from what I'd discovered so far, he too could be dead. Andover seemed to be wiping the trail clean. I felt despair beginning to settle in. Was my search hopeless?

Joy said, 'Roger Brookes committed suicide about a year ago.'

Another surprise. 'Why suicide?' I voiced my thoughts aloud.

Joy shrugged. 'I've no idea. Joe was surprised too.' Her face clouded over again at the memory of her boss. Why hadn't Joe, or even Miles, told me about Brookes? Perhaps Miles didn't know.

My mind was racing. Why had Roger Brookes killed himself? Had Andover got to him again and demanded more money? Had Andover threatened to expose what he knew about Brookes? Had it really been suicide? I needed to speak to Brookes' wife.

'Does his widow still live in Gloucestershire?'

'I don't know. Sorry.'

I'd find out. It meant going there to check. I could hire a car. Having made my decision I returned to the subject of Joe's death.

'What cases was Joe working on?' I asked, hoping that her answer might give me a reason as to why Joe was killed, which didn't have anything to do with Andover or me. I was probably clutching at straws.

I could see Joy running through the files in her mind. After a moment she said, 'There were a couple of divorces, a suspected business fraud and a child abduction case – the father has taken the little boy back to Germany and the mother wants him here in England.'

'Anything that might have upset someone enough to kill him?'

She flinched at my choice of words; her freckled face lost its colour. 'The police asked me that. I told them, there wasn't. They were all the usual.' Which, along with me showing up on the morning of Joe's murder, would have left Crowder with the assumption that Joe's death was connected with me. It didn't need the brains of a professor to work that one out.

The noisy women took the table next to us and started talking about a joint acquaintance, who by all accounts, had really got up their nose by finding herself a very rich husband not six months after the old one had been laid to rest.

'Do you mind if we get a breath of fresh air?' Joy suddenly declared, standing up.

I was all for that. We turned out of the museum and headed east. The sun put in a fleeting appearance between racing white clouds and when it did it felt quite hot, with the promise of summer in its rays. Someone had recently cut the grass in the university grounds opposite. I breathed in the tangy smell thinking that if I could have bottled this and sold it in prison I would have made a fortune, or at least enough to have kept the weirdos and sadists off my back. To me the smell, like that of the sand and sea, represented freedom.

'Who found Joe?' I asked.

'I did, when I arrived for work.'

I snatched a glance at her. She was staring at the pavement.

'He was lying on his back on the floor. His face was blue and there was blood around his mouth. His hands were clenched.'

A minute or so of silence followed. The traffic roared and screeched around us. We turned the corner and headed towards the seafront. 'What was the office like?'

'It had been ransacked, but as far as I could tell nothing was missing.'

'What about my file?' I held my breath.

'That had already been archived.'

'Where?'

'In the big storage warehouse on the Rodney Road industrial estate.'

'And it's still there?'

'I assume so.'

'Did the police ask you about it?'

She shook her head.

Was that because they already knew what it contained? Could Joe have copied it for them? 'Could I see it?' My heart was pounding; what if she said no? How could I gain access to it without her permission?

She said, 'I'll give them a call and tell them you're coming.'

'Thanks,' I said gratefully. 'I'd like to collect it straight away.'

She pulled out her mobile. As she made the call I watched a little boy playing with his father on the common. They were trying to get a kite up. It reminded me of all the times I had played with my sons. I wanted to howl, but instead sought refuge in my anger. I pushed aside all thoughts and feelings of love and replaced them with hatred.

'You can collect it when you're ready,' Joy said, signing off.

I was impatient to get my hands on it. 'Is it all right if I go now?'

'Of course. I think I'll go for a walk along the seafront, clear my head a bit.'

I watched her forlorn figure stroll past a

balding, scruffily dressed man who was sitting on a bench under the trees. He rose and folded his newspaper. Not another of Crowder's men following me, I thought with exasperation.

The warehouse was the other side of Portsmouth. As soon as I could I caught a taxi, but as the warehouseman came towards me with empty hands and a mournful face, I knew at once that my file had gone.

'It was booked out early yesterday morning,' he announced.

'What time?' I cursed under my breath. I should have come sooner.

'Nine-fifteen.'

Probably just after Joe had been killed. 'Who signed for it?'

He peered down at the paperwork. 'Alex Albury.'

I should have guessed. With a racing heart, I said, 'Can I see?'

It was a forgery and not a very good one. I didn't recognise the writing. I hadn't really expected to, perhaps just hoped. The police had no need to fake my signature; they could simply take the file. And they wouldn't have got to it until after Joe's death, which would have been at least an hour or so later. But Andover? That was very different. He must have come immediately after he'd killed Joe. My heart lifted a little. If I had wanted confirmation that Andover was in England then I was getting it.

'Don't you check identity?' I asked, rather crossly.

'I *do*. Dunno if Darren did and he checked it out.'

'Can I talk to Darren?'

'You could if he was here. Didn't come in this morning.'

'Where does he live?'

'Bill, where does Darren live?' he called out.

A silver-haired man popped his head around one of the giant aisles. 'With his mum.'

'Where's that?' I asked, trying to curb my impatience.

'Chatham Road, number sixteen,' Bill answered readily enough; he seemed to lack any curiosity. I thanked them both, gave them a couple of quid each for a beer and headed for Chatham Road.

A woman in her fifties answered the door of a second floor maisonette in a run-down area not far from the football ground. She was balancing a small child on her hip. The little girl looked as though she'd just eaten her way through a Cadbury's chocolate factory. Her mouth, fingers and jumper were covered with the brown stuff.

She was whining softly and the woman looked decidedly cross.

'Yes?' she snapped.

A shapeless beige cardigan hung off her squat figure like a sack; her long denim skirt trailed to her feet, which were bare and dirty, her toenails were too long and she stank of nicotine. Her fingers were yellow and her nails bitten.

'Is Darren there?' I tried to peer around her, but all I could see was a narrow hall with peeling wallpaper and all I could hear was a television set.

'No, he ain't. Who the hell are you?' Her eyes narrowed with suspicion; her lips were like a crack in the pavement.

'His mates from work said I could find him here,' I replied, trying to win her over with my smile. It didn't work.

'They lied then.' She made to shut the door on me but I slammed my hand on it.

'Where is he?' I demanded roughly, recognising that charm school stuff was wasted on her.

'You the filth?' she spat at me.

'Where is he?'

'I don't know. If I did I'd go there and let him deal with his brat.'

The child, as if sensing the woman's hatred, started snivelling louder, which earned her a

'Shut your face.' It only served to make the child cry more. If I could have spared the time I would have felt sorry for the little girl.

'He buggered off down that bleeding pub last night and hasn't been home since,' the woman moaned. 'Probably picked up a slag and is sleeping off a hangover. You wait till I get my hands on him, bloody idle bastard, just like his father.'

'Which pub?' I shouted, above the child's wailing.

'The Whippet and if you find him tell him he's a useless wanker.'

I had passed the Whippet on my way here. Now I headed back there with an uneasy feeling in the pit of my stomach. I pushed open the door and wondered if I'd stumbled into a smokers' convention. If smoking had been banned in public places then no one had told the landlord and occupants here. I had to part the air before I could reach the bar and by then I must have passively smoked about five cigarettes.

The barman, a skinny, small man with thinning brown hair and a face like a ferret, was engaged down the far end of the bar. I glanced around wondering if Darren was here, and if so which of the ten men he might be: one of those with a foot resting on the rail round the bottom of the bar and watching the horse racing on a large flat-screen TV to my right; or perhaps that young one perched on the stool beside them. I ruled out a couple of men playing the gaming machines on account of their fluorescent jackets; they were either binmen or roadmen. Then there was a group playing pool in the far left-hand corner.

'Yes?' the barman said laconically.

'I'm looking for Darren.'

'Don't think we sell that in here. What is it? A new drink?' He gazed around smiling, searching for his audience. Nobody responded.

'Joker, are you?' I said roughly, moving in a little closer and surprising him. Prison had taught me how to act big and menacing. It had also taught me not to show fear. Not that this skinny little runt frightened me. 'Where is he?'

'What's it to you?'

'None of your fucking business. Now, have you seen him?'

The barman hesitated, glancing around as if seeking support, but nobody was the slightest bit interested. 'Not since last night. Probably sleeping off a hangover. He was in here chucking it about as if he'd won the bloody lottery.'

Was he now? I held the barman's stare a moment, then seeing he was telling the truth, I left. I walked slowly back into town. Where was

Darren? Would he show up at home, or was he more likely to appear on the mortuary slab? Had Andover killed him? Darren could identify him. Should I tell the police? They might be able to trace Andover. Even if I did tell them anonymously, it was still too risky. The warehousemen, Darren's mother and that barman would be able to say that I had come asking questions. DCI Crowder already believed I was Andover. I didn't think he would need much persuading that I had lifted my file from the warehouse and killed Darren.

My thoughts had taken me to the central library in Guildhall Square. It was a large three-storey building with a café on the top, and would have many more resources than my small local library in Bembridge, and whilst I was here I thought I might as well continue my research. I had to find Westnam. He was the only one left. I just hoped and prayed he was still alive, and that he hadn't left the country.

The Guildhall clock chimed three as I climbed the steps and it was only then that I realised I was hungry. I hadn't eaten since breakfast. I grabbed a sandwich and a cup of coffee in the café. It was quiet and apart from myself there was only one elderly couple and a young woman who was dressed in a rather eccentric and eclectic

range of clothing. She made me think of my
neighbour, Scarlett and her mother. I didn't recall
Ruby Kingston as one of my mother's friends.
But then why should I? I had left the Island years
ago, firstly to attend university in Sheffield, and
then to work in London before meeting Vanessa
and moving to the Hamble. After the boys were
born we had returned to the Island as a family to
spend August and Christmas there with my
mother. Olivia had had an entirely separate life
from my own, and one I suddenly realised I knew
little about. I wriggled a little uncomfortably at
the memory of my selfishness. I had been so full
of my own self-importance. I should have taken
more interest. I should have been more caring.
With a sip of my rapidly cooling coffee, I thought
I should have told Olivia I loved her. Now it
was too late.

Could I trust the words of a senile old lady
when she said that she'd seen someone push
Olivia down the stairs? Her daughter didn't
believe her, but then her daughter clearly didn't
believe in my innocence. Not that I should blame
her for that. She didn't know me. I did blame
her though.

I finished my coffee and headed for the
Directory of Directors on the assumption that
Westnam might have got another directorship. I

spent the next hour trawling my way online through that and various other directories trying to locate Westnam. He wasn't listed as a company director anywhere. That didn't mean to say he didn't have his own business, it just wasn't a limited company. He could, of course, be operating as a sole trader or partner. He could have gone abroad to live and work.

With irritation I left the library and went to sit in Victoria Park for a few minutes. The breeze was a little on the fresh side but the shining sun, and the luxury of freedom, more than compensated for that. The trees were unfurling tiny fresh green leaves, and the tulips were splendid in their bright yellow and soldier redcoats. How could I find Westnam? I was convinced he could give me the key to all this. Yet if I discovered why Andover had blackmailed him how would that help me? Oh, I could tell the police, but if Westnam didn't know who Andover was, the police would only think that Andover was me, so back to square one. No, I was looking at this the wrong way round. Why had Andover chosen me? That was the question that needed answering.

I could hear the trains screeching across the bridge into Portsmouth station. What if Andover's vendetta against me *had* been personal though? I thought of my mother and Ruby's words. Had my mother known Andover? Was he a friend of the family, a relative even? There was someone who might know.

I glanced at my watch. It was 4.15pm. Before I could change my mind I was heading for the railway station. The London Waterloo train was just pulling in as I stepped onto the platform. Without hesitation I climbed on board and twenty-eight minutes later I was alighting at Petersfield. A brisk walk through the small, but rapidly developing Hampshire market town and I was crossing the park, skirting the lake. Opposite me now was a large detached modern house set back from the road. I stood for some time gazing up at it trying to stifle the resentment inside me. I didn't succeed. I squared my shoulders and sallied forth.

## CHAPTER 6

'What do you want, Alex?' Vanessa's shock at seeing me on her doorstep swiftly gave way to wariness.

She had hardly changed in three years. If anything she looked more attractive, more self-assured than I remembered. I could still see her face during those long days and weeks of my trial as her concern had begun to turn to suspicion. Her expression would haunt and hurt me forever. Then at my mother's funeral she had looked pale and tired. Now her dark curtain of hair was sleek and shining, framing an elfin face as yet unsullied by lines even though she was approaching forty-three. She was slender and I'd forgotten quite how small she was. Always a tidy dresser I could tell her stylish trousers and blouse were expensive. Her appearance and this house confirmed my view that Gus Newberry, her new husband, was doing all right for himself, though at what, I had no idea.

'I want to talk,' I said I hoped evenly, though my stomach was churning. I didn't think I still loved her, but there was something tugging at my heart.

'I'm not sure we've got anything to say to each other.'

'On the contrary we've got a great deal to say. How are *my* sons?' I hadn't intended demanding to see them, but as the train had sped through the countryside, my heart had beat faster at the thought that I might do so. Vanessa's rather frosty reception was only serving to make me more bloody-minded.

'You can't see them. You know what the court said.'

My stomach clenched. Damn Andover to hell and back.

'Besides they're not here,' she quickly added, after seeing my angry expression. 'David is at his fencing class and Philip's at football practice. I'll need to pick them up soon.' She dashed a glance at her watch.

I tried to hide my disappointment. 'Aren't you going to ask me in or is only the doorstep good enough for a man you once said you loved.'

I saw a flash of anger in her hazel eyes. Then she shrugged and turned away leaving me to close the door and follow her down the hall into a spacious kitchen enlarged by a beautifully designed glass extension. I felt envy and bitterness.

There were schoolbooks on the table including Shakespeare's *Othello*. I recalled my English studies at university – what had the great man said about losing one's reputation? Something about it making a man bestial. Maybe he was right because I wanted to smash this fucking perfect room to pieces except for the studio photograph of David and Philip on the wall beside a huge framed genealogy chart, bearing Gus Newberry's name. I felt so sad and sick with regret that I could hardly breathe. My heart was heavy and my arms ached to hold my sons. I would get the bastard who had stitched me up and nail his balls to the wall. I'd find a way to make him suffer as I had suffered, and if I died doing it then so be it. Yes, Shakespeare was right, losing your reputation did make you bestial.

'Have you told them I'm out of prison?'

'Alex. I…' She pushed her hand through her

hair, her expression reflecting her anguish. 'You
do understand. I need to prepare them.'

'For what? The demon father, the ex-convict. I
suppose you and Gus have made me out to be a
cross between the Kray brothers and Ronnie Biggs.'

'There's no need to be so bitter.'

'Isn't there? How would you like to have
almost four years of your life taken from you?
To lose everything you valued, including the
people you loved.'

'I've suffered too.'

'Oh, yes, it looks like it. Vanessa, have you any
idea of what it's like to be locked in a room you
can't break out of? To experience the complete loss
of control over your own destiny, knowing there is
no escape and that you just have to wait. And all
that time you know that you shouldn't be there,
that you are innocent. Only no one believes you.'

'What do you want, Alex?' she demanded.

I guessed her guilt was making her angry,
because she hadn't and probably still didn't
believe in my innocence. I watched her gather
up the exercise books and place them on top of a
cabinet at the side of the room. I took a deep
breath and told myself to get a grip. I needed
information and this wasn't the way to get it. In
prison I had dreamt of the day when I would see
her again, rehearsing what I would say; it would

veer from pleading with her to believe in my innocence, to berating her for her callousness in deserting me, now all those words were useless.

'I haven't come here to argue with you, or score points,' I begun.

'No!' She spun round her cheeks flushed with anger. Her eyes flashing.

'I've come for information.' And the hope of seeing my sons, I said to myself.

Her anger gave way to bafflement, then suspicion. 'About what?'

I guessed she thought I was going to ask about Gus. 'About my mother.'

'Oh!'

'Was there any indication that she might have been pushed down the stairs?'

She looked surprised. 'No. Why, should there be? There was a loose stair rod, the carpet had come away, her slipper caught it and she fell.'

'Did she ever say anything to you before she died, about being worried or frightened?' I could see my question confused her.

'What is this, Alex?'

'Did the police ever hint at her death being suspicious?'

'No.'

Her small pointed face puckered up with a frown. I could see that she was wondering if I'd gone completely mad. Perhaps she thought I had developed a persecution complex. I persisted.

'It's important, Vanessa.'

She decided to humour me; probably thinking it would be quicker that way to get rid of me.

'She called me a couple of times, before she died, asking for you. I tried to tell her that you weren't here but she wasn't listening, or couldn't quite take it in. She was a little confused.'

'What did she say?'

'I can't recall exactly. It was a long time ago now. She had a bee in her bonnet about things being moved, but I think she must have just mislaid them.'

'What kind of things?'

'Books, jewellery, ornaments.'

'Did she mention if any strangers had called on her? Or if she thought someone had been in the house?'

'Alex…' Vanessa said exasperated.

'Did she?' I pressed.

Vanessa sighed heavily. 'On a couple of occasions she thought she had burglars, but nothing was ever taken.'

'How do you know? You weren't there.'

'No, and neither were you.'

'I don't think you need to remind me of that,' I snapped.

'Don't make me feel any more guilty than I already do. I should have done more for Olivia. I liked her.'

There was a brief fragile silence. 'Did she report it to the police?'

'She might have done. She didn't say. I'm not sure she wanted to involve them after what happened.'

No, and I doubted whether they would have believed her anyway.

'Why this interest, Alex?'

I told her what Ruby Kingston had said.

'I remember her and her daughter, Scarlett. 'Bit of a weird girl, dressed like a hippy and very surly. I never did trust her.'

'You knew her?' I asked, unable to hide my surprise.

'I thought she might be Olivia's phantom mover of objects. I tackled her about it. She went right off the deep end.'

That sounded like my neighbour. 'Why her?'

'She was your mother's cleaner.'

Now I was surprised. Why hadn't Scarlett told me? Still we'd hardly had much of a conversation, and I knew she didn't approve of me.

Vanessa continued, 'I dismissed her as soon as Olivia died. Then I had the locks changed. Her father was a thief. Spent years in and out of prison.'

A pain stabbed at my heart with Vanessa's cruel and thoughtless words. Now I was beginning to understand Scarlett's hostility towards me. She probably blamed me for getting the sack.

Keeping my voice steady, I said, 'Because her father was a thief then she must be a thief too, is that it?'

'Of course not, I…'

'Doesn't bode well for our sons then,' I said harshly.

'I didn't mean…' She flushed, angrily and guiltily.

'I'd have expected more generosity and open mindedness from you, Vanessa.'

'Don't give me that, Alex. It hasn't been easy.'

My life hasn't exactly been a picnic either, I thought of replying, but didn't. Two things then happened, the telephone rang and the front door opened.

Vanessa snatched up the phone and, with a backward glance at me that said 'stay', she hurried out into the hall. I heard whispers. A few seconds later Gus Newberry walked into the kitchen. He wore a smile and a dark pin-striped suit. You could almost see your reflection in the shine of his shoes and even after a hard day at the office he still looked as if he'd just left home. He was shorter and broader than I had imagined and older, or perhaps he just looked older. His hair was straight, short, iron grey and wiry. He wore a pair of steel-rimmed glasses. I put him in his late forties.

I could see at a glance that he was an intelligent man who was sizing me up quickly and competently with sharp penetrating eyes between deep frown lines on a face too narrow to be classed as good-looking but nevertheless had a certain quality of attractiveness about it. After a moment he said, 'Beer?'

'I don't think I'm staying,' I said surprised at his offer and jerked my head at the hall where Vanessa was talking into the telephone.

'She'll be a while yet. You've got time for one beer and then I'll run you back to the station.'

'Thanks,' I muttered. I wanted to hate him but he was making it difficult for me to do so. There didn't seem anything to hate about him. He looked and sounded like he would be a good father to my boys. Despite that, it should have been me, not him, raising my sons.

He crossed to the fridge, handed me a bottle of beer and waved me into a seat. He settled himself opposite. I expected him to at least remove his jacket and loosen his tie, like any other man would have done the moment he came in, but Gus seemed perfectly at home in formal attire in the immaculate kitchen.

'Have you any idea why someone wanted to frame you?' His voice was authoritative with a hint of warmth. 'You *were* set up.'

'Pity Vanessa didn't believe that.' He didn't flinch at my icy tone.

'You must look at it from her point of view: the case was investigated by officers at the highest level, a private detective and your lawyers could find nothing to contradict the evidence. What choice did she have? But her heart said you hadn't done it.'

Then why divorce me I felt like saying?

Gus removed his spectacles and polished them. 'I take it you're trying to find out who set you up.'

It wasn't so much a question as a statement. It was my turn to let my expression do the talking. I could hear Vanessa trying to end her conversation; it sounded as if she was talking to her mother who had always been impossible to get rid of.

Gus said, 'What chance do you think you'll have of succeeding?'

My head came up. I didn't like his tone but his expression was neutral.

'Alex, you are dealing with a very clever man. I suspect he knows your every move before you've even made it.'

I thought of Joe and my missing file, of Darren, and the aeroplane incident. I even thought of that woman in Brading Church and her veiled warning. Gus was right. It was as if someone could foretell what I was going to do.

Vanessa walked in. 'You're home early,' she said to Gus, throwing me a nervous look.

'I'll take Alex to the station.'

At the door Vanessa said, 'You won't contact the boys, will you, Alex? I don't want them upset. They've got exams and…'

'I won't contact them, not yet.' I didn't mean it as a threat though I realised it must have sounded like one.

I glimpsed down at the hall table as Gus picked up his car keys. There was a message on a note pad for Gus to call someone called Rodney, an electric bill, a bank statement, and a renewal form for a pilot's licence. That brought me up with a start. I didn't know Gus could fly an aeroplane. But then why should I? I hardly knew anything about the man Vanessa had married three months after our divorce.

We didn't speak again until we arrived at the station when Gus offered his hand and said, 'Good luck.'

On the train and the hovercraft home I went over my conversation with him; one phrase stuck in my mind. *'You are dealing with a very clever man. I suspect he knows your every move before you've even made it.'* Was that a warning? I hadn't thought so when he had said it, but now I wasn't so sure. I couldn't get that pilot's licence out of my mind. Where had Gus been when that aeroplane was dive-bombing me? I should find out. Not that I thought he was Andover. Vanessa hadn't met him until after I'd been in prison for eight months.

The gate to the houseboat squeaked as I pushed it back. A sudden swish of noise came from behind me as I stepped into the forecourt. Before I had time to register what it was, my arms were pinned behind me in a tight grip and a voice hissed in my ear.

'Make a noise and I break both arms. Understand?'

I nodded.

'Good, now let's go inside and have a quiet talk, shall we?'

In the circumstances it seemed the most sensible thing to do.

# CHAPTER 7

'I gather you've been looking for me?' He stabbed at the light before releasing me. I turned to face him. 'Clive Westnam,' he announced.

This time my prison training couldn't keep the surprise from my face. He looked nothing like his newspaper photographs. He was much thinner, his face was gaunt and the sleekness of power had sloughed off him. The luxuriant silver hair was now thin and greasy and his clothes, an old anorak over a pullover and a pair of suit trousers, were grubby and creased. His shoes were down at heel and scuffed. I thought life had treated me harshly in prison but wherever he had been it hadn't been much better.

'Not the man you remember, eh?'

'Who is?' I replied harshly.

'Prison doesn't seem to have harmed you; except for the hair you look about the same, perhaps fitter. Bloody holiday inside, whilst your victims have suffered you've been living the life of Riley.'

'I would hardly say that.'

'Then what would you say?' He thrust his face close to mine but eased back almost immediately when I didn't react. I'd been frightened by harder men than him. He was a pussycat compared to the psychos who had wanted a piece of me in prison. He could see that he would be no match for me. I was younger and much fitter. If he wanted a fight I could give him one.

'I didn't take your money,' I said evenly.

He laughed bitterly. 'Oh, come on. I'm not the bloody law.'

'Did you ever meet me?' I pressed.

'You know damn well I didn't. You called me. It was your voice and you sent me those e-mails. You threatened me.'

'With what?' I stepped forward. I could see the wariness in his eyes.

'I thought I was giving to charity. You conned me.'

'Someone conned us both. What did Andover have on you?'

'Nothing.' A flash of anger, but it was bluster.

'Oh, come on, he had something on all three of you, otherwise you would never have agreed to hand the money over.'

'I was a company chairman. I had a good job. I had a wife and a lovely house until you came into my life and now I've got fuck all.'

I felt like saying join the club. There was one difference between us, I knew I was innocent and I knew that Westnam had a secret that he didn't want exposed.

'I want my money back, Albury. I'm going to see that you pay up.'

'And how are you going to do that?' I said with a mixture of cockiness and anger. Westnam's eyes flicked beyond me but before I could react a voice said:

'He isn't, I am.'

I spun round. I hadn't heard or sensed anyone enter, but behind me were two men, one of whom I recognised instantly from my days in Brixton prison. My heart sank and with it came fear. Despite that I forced myself to show little reaction and to keep my voice even when I said,

'Hello, Rowde.' I managed to hold his stare, which was difficult because I knew the evil that this man was capable of. I'd been on the receiving end of it many times and had witnessed it being inflicted on others. With Rowde's appearance the prison smell was back in my nostrils.

'It's good to see you again, Alex,' Rowde replied. He was the slimmer and smaller of the two men.

'I wish I could say the same of you,' I said casually, yet meaning every word of it.

He laughed and strode across the room as if he owned it whilst his henchman, a square-set man with eyes like scratched marbles and an expression to match, blocked the door.

'Nice place you've got here.' Rowde sat down.

Westnam was looking smug but nervous. I could see beads of sweat on his brow. I hoped and prayed there would be none on mine. If I allowed my mind to go back to the time when I had shared a cell with this man, before my transfer to Camp Hill, I would break out in a cold sweat and perspire so heavily he'd think I'd just stepped out of the shower.

'Got anything to drink?' Rowde crossed his legs and relaxed into the seat. In contrast to Westnam he was expensively but casually dressed in a lightweight Henri Lloyd sailing jacket over a navy cotton polo neck, and khaki-coloured jeans. He looked as if he had just stepped off a powerful and expensive motorboat. His hair was short and dark with only a few flecks of grey. He was about my age and had put on a bit of weight around the midriff since his release from prison. Apart from that he was the man I remembered, the man who had terrorised me for six months.

'I'll fetch some beer.'

'No, Westnam will do that.'

'It's below, in the kitchen.'

Westnam scurried away.

'You've got him well trained.' I sat down opposite Rowde, trying to emulate his relaxed manner, yet fearing what might come next. Whatever it would be I doubted it would be very pleasant, for me anyway.

'He was easier than you.'

'Yeah, and I've still got the scars to prove it.'

'You always were a stubborn bugger. You know what we've come for.'

'I haven't got it and I don't know where it is.'

'Same old story. I would have thought you'd have learned by now that I don't like lies and I don't like liars. Neither does Barry.' He jerked his head in the direction of marble man.

My mind was racing. How could I get out of this? Where were the police when you needed them? If they were keeping surveillance on me then why the hell had they let this masochist and his thug walk in? But I could answer that question myself: to see where it might lead them. The police couldn't demand money with menace but they could let someone else do it and then arrive to take the glory and the money.

'I'm sorry to disappoint you both. I was framed.'

'So you keep saying. I hope you're not going to bore me again.'

I didn't answer. There was nothing I could say. Westnam was taking his time fetching that beer and I guessed he was having a quick one whilst he was down there. I didn't blame him. If he was looking for the money though he was going to be disappointed.

Rowde continued. 'Westnam will be very upset if you don't give him back his million and so will I. He's going to give me a commission for helping him.'

'Does he know that?'

'Of course.' Rowde leaned forward and lowered his voice, 'But he doesn't know how much.'

Poor sod, I thought.

Rowde laughed as Westnam appeared with two cans of beer. He handed one to Rowde who took it but didn't drink from it. He held it carefully in his slim hands.

'Has he told you where it is?' Westnam said.

'He will.'

'You don't trust this bastard, do you?' I threw at Westnam.

'Why shouldn't I?'

'Why should you?' I rejoined. 'If I had the money, and told you where to get it, do you seriously think he'll let you keep it?'

Westnam threw a nervous glance at Rowde.

Rowde stood up. 'I think it's time we stopped all this polite chit chat and got down to some business.'

I saw him nod at marble man and resisted both the temptation to turn round and to stand up. I tried to keep my body language and expression as relaxed as possible which was difficult when I was shit scared.

'I want that money, Alex, and I'm going to get it.'

Marble man was now beside his boss, towering over him both in height and girth and making Rowde look like a weakling. It made me wonder for a moment how Rowde could be so feared both inside and outside prison. Marble man looked like a thug who would have no compunction in beating a man to death, whereas

Rowde looked as though he wouldn't harm a fly. But Rowde was clever. He was a manipulator. He had charm and good looks. He was plausible. He spun his web and you got caught in it if you weren't careful. You confided in him. You trusted him. Then he used you and your secrets to get you exactly where he wanted. He was completely without conscience, remorse or guilt.

I said, 'I suppose you could try beating it out of me, but I'd either give you a false trail to get you off my back, or I'd die and then neither you nor Westnam would get any money. A bit pointless, wouldn't you say?'

'Couldn't agree with you more, Alex, which is why we're not going to do that.'

He picked up the photograph of David and Philip and the blood froze in my veins. I dug my fingers into the palms of my hands so hard that the knuckles turned white. Westnam, holding his beer, looked like a rabbit caught in the glare of car headlamps. Marble man smiled at me. I could have kicked his teeth down his throat, but that's what he would have liked me to try, and with three of them I didn't like the odds. I wasn't going to win whichever way you looked at it.

'Nice-looking boys,' Rowde said.

I remained silent.

'You wouldn't want anything to happen to

them. Be a pity to see those pretty faces scarred for life.'

I leapt forward but marble man put a great big paw on my chest.

'Leave them alone,' I hissed.

'I wouldn't dream of hurting them, *normally,* but these aren't normal times, are they, Alex? You have something I want. And these boys are something you want. I'm prepared to do a deal. You get me the money and the boys stay unharmed. And don't think I don't know where they are because I know exactly where they live and where they go to school. Getting to them is child's play, if you'll excuse the pun.' He gave an evil smile.

I ran a hand through my hair. 'For Christ's sake, Rowde, how many times do I have to tell you I don't have the money. It was a scam, a fit-up, a frame.'

'Then you'd better find out who did it and ask him for the money.'

'What do you think I'm trying to do?' I almost screeched. 'When I find the money you can have it with pleasure.'

But Rowde shook his head. 'I'm afraid that's not good enough. I need it now and so does Mr Westnam. You've got seven days, Alex, until next Tuesday morning, 8am.'

'How the fuck can I get it for you when I don't know where it is!'

'That's your problem. Perhaps your rich lawyer friend will loan it to you. And I wouldn't bother going to the police, that would make me and Barry very unhappy; so unhappy that I would have to take revenge.'

He threw the photograph onto the floor and ground his heel into it smashing the glass. I made to surge forward feeling as if he'd physically wounded my boys, but marble man held me back.

'It just slipped right out of my hand,' Rowde said. 'Seven days, Alex, then I'll be back for the money or your boys get that treatment for real. I promise you that and you know I always keep my promises.'

Only too well, I thought, recalling the beatings he'd arranged for me to take in prison. I nodded.

Rowde smiled. 'That wasn't so difficult, was it? I'm glad you've come to your senses. Now I think it's time we were leaving. Thanks for the beer but I'm not thirsty.' He poured the contents over the photograph, threw the can down and stamped on it. I felt as though he was stamping on my heart.

He brushed past me with Westnam in tow. I saw Rowde nod briefly at marble man and tried to tense myself for the blow that was to come but it made no difference, it still hurt like hell. He knew just where to strike, on the lower left hand side of my back. I went down like a sack of potatoes. His boot came into my kidneys. I screamed in pain, and again it came. I felt my head being pulled up by the hair and then wrenched back with his punch. I tasted the hot sticky blood as it ran out of my mouth.

'And here's one for luck, just to remind you of what your boys might suffer.'

Another kick in the gut. Then the lights went out. It was black and deep and it swallowed me up.

## CHAPTER 8

When I opened my eyes it felt as though someone had inserted a red-hot poker up my nose and singed my brain. It was some time later when I tried again. This time the poker was still there but it wasn't quite so hot. I was staring up at the ceiling. How many weeks had passed since I'd entered prison? I had no coherent memory to draw on. My recollections of people, procedures and prison were just a jumble in my head, as unreal as a dream, or rather nightmare. They had no substance. It was as if I were watching it from the outside, a near death experience. That was me going through reception, lying on my narrow prison bed, eating prison food off plastic trays with plastic cutlery, but it wasn't me. Perhaps I was inside someone else's head. This wasn't happening. It couldn't be.

'You're awake then?'

Since when had they allowed women into my prison? I swivelled my eyes and with a start saw my neighbour, Scarlett, sitting beside my bed. I frowned, then wished I hadn't. The poker had friends; tiny needles shot through my head.

'How are you feeling?'

A hell of a lot better now I know I'm not in prison I nearly replied, but stopped myself. I found the roof of my mouth and said: 'I'll live.'

She looked pleased, which surprised me. Her brown eyes softened and she smiled. A first. She should do it more often, I thought. She was quite attractive. Vanessa had been unkind in her remarks. Scarlett simply didn't conform when it came to clothes and appearance. Her hair was streaked with a myriad of different hues, including blue and green this time and she was wearing a loose-fitting floral blouse over a long multicoloured skirt.

'Where am I?' I struggled to sit up. A stab of pain caught me by surprise. I winced and gritted my teeth. The room swam before me, and Scarlett's concerned expression deepened. She surged forward to prevent me from doing whatever she thought I intended to do, but I waved her away and held my position with my body propped up against the bedstead. The pain eased.

'St Mary's Hospital, Newport.'

I was in a small ward of just four beds and daylight was streaming in through the windows. Then it came back to me. I sat bolt upright with a scream, which I somehow managed to stifle before it disturbed the whole of the ward. This time the pain wasn't only physical but emotional. My boys. I had to stop Rowde from hurting them, killing them even, because I had no doubt that he would. He would probably have me watch it too. I must have turned a peculiar colour because Scarlett leapt up and said, 'I'm going to call the nurse.'

'No. Please,' I managed to whisper with enough conviction and determination to make her hover. Why was she bothering with me? Why was she even here? 'I'm all right, just give me a moment.' A moment was all I had. I had already lost a night lying here. God, it was only one night, wasn't it?

'How long have I been here?' I asked anxiously.

'About ten hours. I found you on the floor of your houseboat. I'd lost Mother again.' She glared at me. Now I saw that where other women blushed and got upset, Scarlett simply scowled or glared.

She added, 'I saw those men leave your houseboat so I knew you were still awake. When you didn't answer I thought you might be avoiding me, but the door sort of swung open and I found you on the floor. I called the ambulance.'

'You didn't call the police?' I asked, watching her carefully. She returned my gaze.

'No.'

She could see I had been beaten up. From what Vanessa had told me though, I guessed that she had probably been raised with a deep mistrust of the police because of her father. I was warming towards Scarlett.

'Why not?' I asked.

'It's none of my business,' she shrugged.

'Then what are you doing here?' It sounded ungrateful but I didn't mean it that way. I wondered if she'd take umbrage like she usually did. This time she didn't.

'I had to bring Mother into the day centre. It's all right – I found her last night. As I was here, I thought I'd call in and see how you were at the same time. Besides,' she added, 'I owe you for finding Mum the other evening and bringing her home.'

'You're welcome.' I winced and held my side as I tried to propel myself up. 'You've got a car?'

'Yes.'

'Good, you can give me a lift into Newport.'

'But you can't possibly…OK, but don't blame me if you have a relapse,' she hotly declared.

'I wouldn't dream of it. Where are my clothes?' Seven days, Rowde had given me. This was day one. By next Tuesday I had to find Andover and that money. Time was a luxury I no longer had.

'In the cabinet.'

She left me to get dressed which I did as swiftly and as silently as I could. It wasn't easy. My body screamed out in pain, which I had to ignore. I couldn't feel anything, not yet. And I couldn't rest up until I had found Andover. A nurse showed up with a stern expression on her face.

'And just where do you think you're going?'

'Home,' I told her curtly. 'I'm discharging myself. I'll sign any papers you give me to relieve you of any guilt, or comeback if I have a relapse, but I must get out of here.'

She stared at me for a moment, then with a lift of her eyebrows turned swiftly on her heel and left me to finish dressing. Putting on my socks and shoes involved such a supreme effort that I almost fainted. I gritted my teeth, remembered the broken photograph of my sons on the floor of the houseboat and foresaw their broken bodies dumped in a dank ditch somewhere, and it was amazing what I could achieve. I was like Superman after recovering from a dose of Kryptonite.

Amid many censorious looks I signed the forms and found Scarlett waiting for me by the lifts. We didn't speak until we had reached her car, a rather rusty old Renault, but as long as it went it could have been a Mark One Ford for all I cared.

With much grunting and groaning I eased myself into the passenger seat. I scanned the road behind us looking for marble man. I couldn't see him. Of course there was no need for him to follow me now; Rowde knew where I lived and how to get to my sons. He had wound me up like a clockwork toy and had let me go. I just hoped it wouldn't be round and round in circles until I ran out of time, energy and clues. Sometime before the seven days were up I knew Rowde would return to remind me that my time, or rather my sons' time, was running out.

I looked at my reflection in the small mirror. I was not a pretty sight. My face was bruised and swollen and my mouth cut. Miraculously my teeth were still all present, though I thought a couple in the top right hand corner felt a bit loose. Time for the dentist later, I hoped. God alone knew what Scarlett thought of me. I glanced at her as she headed towards the centre of Newport. She'd not asked me any questions and I wondered why. She was remarkably uncurious for a woman.

She must have sensed my gaze because her eyes flittered to me and then back on the road.

'Don't you want to know what happened?' I said.

'I can see what happened. You got beaten up by those men I saw leaving the boat.' She said it so matter of factly that it annoyed me.

'So this is such a regular occurrence for you that you take it in your stride?' I quipped.

'What am I supposed to do? Wail and wring my hands, ask you to tell me why you got beaten up? Firstly I don't wail and wring my hands, and secondly if I did ask, you wouldn't tell me, so there's no point, is there?'

I couldn't fault her reasoning and rather admired it. I guess her father had trained her well. 'What did you tell them at the hospital?'

'That you got beaten up defending my honour.'

'And they believed that?'

'I doubt it, but I think they're too busy to play social worker these days.'

The traffic lights turned red. Even that seemed an unnecessary delay to me. I wanted to scream at them. I wanted Scarlett to ignore them and race through. Every second counted.

I urged myself to calm down. Getting angry wasn't going to achieve anything. Perhaps I should tell Gus. Perhaps he could take the boys away to safety. Yes, maybe that was what I should do. I didn't want to worry Vanessa but I couldn't see her letting Gus take David and Philip out of school without an explanation. And I didn't quite trust him. That pilot's licence still niggled away at me. I needed to know more about Gus Newberry.

Even if I could get my boys to safety I had a terrible feeling that Rowde would find them. I didn't fool myself that marble man was Rowde's only accomplice. Men like Rowde had a whole network of them. I knew that from my days spent with him in prison.

I couldn't tell Scarlett about Rowde or my boys, but I could use this time to ask about my mother.

'Why didn't you tell me you used to clean for my mother?'

'Why should I?'

'Did my mother ever tell you that she thought

someone was in the house? Or that she suspected an intruder?'

Scarlett flashed me a wary look. 'No.'

'And you never saw anyone suspicious loitering around or heard anyone?'

'No. And I'm not a thief.'

'I never said you were. Did you tell the police what Ruby said?'

'About someone pushing Olivia down the stairs? Of course not. Mum doesn't know what she's saying. Your mother fell. It was a tragic accident and I'm sorry. I liked her. '

'So did I,' I muttered.

'Despite your ex wife giving me the push I'm still working at Bembridge House. I clean for Mrs Aslett three times a week.'

The new owner. I'd never met her.

'The rest of the week I work as a chambermaid at the Windmill Hotel, OK?'

'What you do for a living, Scarlett, is nothing to do with me.'

'No, it's not.'

She dropped me off, then chugged away, her exhaust rattling.

An hour later, after a few wary looks and some persuading that I wasn't a reckless driver or a car thief, I had hired a car. It was an automatic, which would save me the physical pain of moving my leg to change gear. I returned to the houseboat and hastily packed a bag and collected the press cutting file, Joe's reports and my notebook. Then I knocked at Scarlett's door. Whilst I waited for her to answer I looked around. There were no cars loitering in the car parks further along the road towards the Toll Gate café, or in the other direction towards the marina, but a few passed me on the Embankment Road. Any one of them could have contained one of Rowde's cronies or the police, which reminded me…had Miles found out what unit DCI Crowder was attached to? Time to call him later. I was just beginning to think that Scarlett was out when the door opened. She looked as though she'd been asleep. She ran a hand through her hair.

'I'm going over to the mainland. I'm not sure when I'll be back. I thought you ought to know in case your mother tries to get on the boat and gets upset.'

'Oh.' She looked surprised. I suppose my thoughtfulness disarmed her.

'Do you have a telephone?' Now I really had surprised her.

'A mobile, why?'

'Give me the number.'

She did without question and again I marvelled at her complete lack of curiosity. It was only when

I was on the car ferry heading across the Solent that I rumbled. She had been with someone, a boyfriend perhaps, judging by the dishevelled appearance, the reluctance to invite me in, and the hastily dragged on clothes. I hadn't seen or heard anyone but I was convinced she hadn't been alone. I was surprised to find it peeved me a little.

I grabbed a sandwich and coffee on the ferry. Eating it was a bit uncomfortable and I drew some peculiar looks from the other passengers who studiously avoided me. That suited me fine. They probably had me down for a thug. Still that was their problem not mine. I called Miles, who confirmed that Crowder was from the Specialist Investigations Unit of the Hampshire Constabulary. There had been no call from Jennifer Clipton. I didn't tell him about Rowde, or Westnam, or that I was on my way to see Brookes' widow. I was taking a bit of a gamble but it was time I talked to her. I just hoped she was still at the address Joe had given me.

She was. As she opened the door to me two hours later, her shocked expression at my bruised face turned to wariness and she closed the door slightly. I could see that she didn't recognise me.

'I'm sorry to trouble you, but I'm looking for Roger Brookes,' I began pleasantly.

'He's not here.' She frowned, puzzlement accompanying wariness. She hadn't changed much from her appearances in court alongside her husband. Still very slim, narrow-hipped and long-legged, bottle blonde straight shoulder-length hair, lines around her blue eyes and tight, slightly hard mouth.

'When will he be back?' I asked in all innocence of his recent demise.

'He won't, he's… he passed away two years ago.'

I feigned horror and shock. It must have worked because her expression softened. I said, 'I'm terribly sorry. I didn't know. Are you his wife?'

She nodded.

'Please forgive me. I do hope I haven't upset you. I had no idea that Roger had died,' I lied, hoping that I looked distraught. Maybe if I came through this I could turn to acting, I thought wryly, as she certainly seemed convinced.

'Were you a friend of his? I don't think I recall you although you do look vaguely familiar.'

'I expect it's hard to recognise me through all the bruises. I had a car accident a couple of days ago. Nothing too serious but enough to make me look like this. I've just come from the States and I forgot I was driving on the wrong side of the road. My name's Bob Morley. I used to work with Roger.'

'Would you like to come in, Mr Morley?'

'I'm not disturbing you?' I stepped inside a wide hall with a highly polished floor and an oak staircase leading up to a galleried landing.

'No, it's nice to have the company. Come through to the kitchen. Would you like a drink?'

'Thanks – and it's Bob. This really is very kind of you. What a lovely house, Roger always was very ambitious.'

She tossed me a smile over her shoulder as she filled the kettle. 'Tea or coffee or perhaps –'

'Tea thanks.'

'How did you know Roger?'

'We worked together years ago at Seatons, the travel company. Then I went to the States and Roger started his own company. I believe he was very successful.' I knew Brookes' background and that of the other three victims by heart. 'How did he die?'

She turned away to make the tea but also to avoid looking at me. 'Suicide.'

When she turned back I could see the anguish on her face. I felt a little sorry for her. But I hardened my heart. I had a job to do and whatever it took I would do it.

I said. 'Maybe I had better go if this is too

painful for you.' Of course it worked.

'No, please. It helps to talk, or so they tell me.'

'What happened? Was the business in trouble?'

'On the contrary, we were doing extremely well, better than ever. Roger got depressed and couldn't get out of it, midlife crisis, I suppose. Who knows?' She handed me my tea. She knew all right. I could tell. 'Help yourself to sugar.'

I declined. I remained silent hoping that she would fill the void. She did.

'I suppose it had something to do with the fraud.'

'Fraud!'

'Oh, not by Roger. He was conned by a very clever man, who got one million pounds out of us and two other businessmen before the police discovered what he was up to. We were OK financially, even though we never got the money back, and I thought Roger was over it, but it must have preyed on his mind.'

'But why did Roger give away one million pounds? Was he being blackmailed?' I asked as innocently as I could. I got a reaction all right and it told me the truth. Her eyes narrowed and her body language stiffened, she lowered her head and took a sip of her tea, avoiding my glance.

'Of course not,' she replied tetchily. 'It was a charitable donation, only there was no charity.'

'That was clumsy and rude of me. I didn't mean to imply there was anything shady or wrong in Roger's business or private life, I just know how these things work. A deal gets done that is OK but not strictly legit, some past aggrieved employee gets hold of it and before you know it you're covering your tracks and someone's got you by the balls.'

She gave a strained smile.

'The police caught this man though?' I asked.

She put down her cup. 'Yes. James Andover was the name he used. His real name was Alexander Albury. He went to prison but he wouldn't say where the money was.' She began fiddling with a gold bracelet, then she looked at her watch. I could tell she was regretting letting me in.

'And did Albury say why he had picked on Roger?'

'Because he was wealthy, I suppose.'

'So are lots of people but they aren't targeted. There must be a connection, so did the police find one?'

Now she was looking at me a little suspiciously. ' No. Besides what does it matter? It's over now, Albury is in prison and Roger's dead.'

I nodded and sipped my tea. 'I wonder if he'll do it again when he comes out of prison? Pick on some other unsuspecting victim that is. I hope he doesn't come back to you,' I mused.

She looked alarmed. 'But surely that won't happen. He'll have learnt his lesson.'

'People rarely learn, and the police can't be everywhere. If he's that clever then maybe next time he won't get caught.'

She rose abruptly and said, 'I'm really sorry, Bob, but I didn't realise how late it was. I've got to go out.'

'It's me who should be apologising for taking up so much of your time and for upsetting you.'

She ushered me out of the door quicker than a kitchen salesman. I had stirred up something and now all I had to do was sit back and see which way she ran.

It was to a house outside Tetbury, about a half hour's drive away. I was prevented from driving up to the front door because the house was set back from the road, squatting very nicely in its own ground and reached by a sweeping gravel driveway.

I left the car in a country lane that bordered the northern side of the new golden-stone manor house and walked the two hundred yards or so around the corner to the east-facing entrance. After gazing right and left like some furtive detective in an old black and white movie I slipped up the driveway and ran across the damp grass until I skirted the back of the house, praying that whoever owned it didn't also own large dogs, or any dogs come to that, which would alert the occupants. But everything remained silent.

I had seen an expensive Range Rover parked at the front of the house by the double garage, beside Emma Brookes' Saab, and as she was nowhere to be seen and hadn't come out of the house, I guessed that whoever lived here was at home.

I walked around the house peering in at the windows. I didn't know what reason I would give for following Emma here, if she challenged me, but I'd find one. I'd tell her the truth if I needed to.

She was in the sitting room, at the back of the house, talking to a younger version of herself. Neither woman seemed remotely interested in what was happening in the garden. I pressed myself against the wall with my head peering around the edge of the French windows like Philip Marlowe on a job, hoping to pick up some of their conversation. The day was still warm and the French door was slightly ajar. I couldn't quite catch everything they said but snatches of it were enough to make my heart quicken.

'No one knows,' hissed the younger woman,

a tall, leggy blonde in her mid twenties, not unattractive but not my type.

'If this Bob Morley is right, he could be out of prison and coming back for more.'

'Then we must stop him.'

'How?'

The next bit I missed as they walked away from the window. Damn. I eased myself round a little more to see what they were doing, hoping perhaps to lip-read. It was a foolish hope, but when you're desperate hope is sometimes all you've got, as I knew only too well. I took a chance. They might see me but I didn't give a toss.

'Don't be daft, Joanne, we can't do that.'

'Jamie could. Do you want to lose all this and see me in prison too?' the daughter retorted, anger turning her fair face ugly.

Emma Brookes' body slumped. 'God, what a mess.'

'Mum, it'll be all right.'

But the look her mother gave her was one of irritation and anger.

'That's what you said last time and look where it's got us. For goodness sake, Joanne, isn't it enough that your father killed himself?'

'You can't blame me for that,' Joanne said hotly.

Emma looked as if she'd like to. 'If you hadn't

got mixed up with Jamie in the first place then none of this would have happened.'

'Well, it did and it's over now.'

Emma looked sceptical. 'Is it, Joanne?' she said quietly.

Her daughter frowned and turned away.

I leaned forward eagerly only to find my arm twisted up behind my back. With a sinking heart I was spun round expecting to find myself looking directly into the face of a uniformed police constable. Instead I was facing a man in his early thirties with a broad face, cropped fair hair, cool blue-grey eyes and very expensive designer clothes rather spoilt by his obvious colour blindness and lack of style.

'And who the fuck are you?' he declared hotly.

'I rather think that ought to be my line,' I said boldly, my gaze unwavering and hoping that my expression showed mild interest when really my mind was racing to find a way out of this and get him to relax his grip on my aching body.

'Not when you're trespassing on my land, it isn't.' He tightened his grip. Judging by the look of him he could and would add another bruise or two to my face and torso, if he thought it was required.

'I'm Bob Morley. I followed Emma Brookes here.' That shook him. The truth usually did.

*When you need to lie always taint it with the truth.*
*That way the suckers will believe you*, one of Ray's.

'Why the fuck should you do that?'

'To see where she went, and do you mind letting me go?' I could see that he was tossing up whether to tell me to go soak my head or do as I ask. Then wariness crept into his suspicion. He released his grip on me.

'You a cop?'

'No.'

Now his expression registered relief, which intrigued me and set my mind racing.

'Who smashed up your face?' he said.

'A Mercedes. I had an accident.' He looked as though he didn't believe me. But then maybe he'd smashed a few faces himself and recognised the pattern. He was prevented from asking any more questions because as we'd been talking the women must have seen us and were now standing before us.

'Jamie, I...'

'Joanne, this…'

The daughter and thug began speaking at the same time. I smiled an apology at Emma and said, humbly, 'I followed you.'

She started and looked nervous whilst her daughter looked livid.

'Why the hell should you do that?' It was Joanne who recovered first.

I addressed my answer to Emma. 'Because you seemed upset and I wanted to know more about Roger's death.'

'Are you another bloody private detective?' Joanne shouted. 'Because if you are there's nothing to tell you. Now piss off.'

Was she was referring to Joe Bristow? She'd given me an idea. Time for some serious lying.

'Joanne is right. I am a private detective. Joe Bristow and I worked together on the Andover case and when Joe was killed, I decided to take over and find out why someone would want to kill him.'

They all look surprised. Jamie glared at me sceptically; I could see his brain ticking over.

'You didn't get that from any Mercedes.' He pointed at my face.

'Joe didn't seem to think that your father's death was suicide.'

Emma turned pale and Joanne bright red whilst Jamie simply looked confused.

'Why wouldn't it be suicide?' Joanne declared petulantly.

'You tell me.'

'There is nothing to tell?'

'No?'

'My father's dead. Now sod off and leave us alone.'

I felt like telling her that frowns that deep would only give her wrinkles.

'Did you know that Alex Albury is out of prison? He might come back to you for more money, or tell what he knows.'

'We can deal with him,' Jamie said, and I had no doubts that he could. He was glaring at me as if he wished he could squash my head between two bricks and then cement it into a wall, but I'd dealt with tougher men than him.

'We?'

'He won't get anything from us,' Joanne said.

'He did before and I'd like to know why?'

'Look…' Jamie stepped menacingly closer to me, but I held my ground.

I turned to Emma. 'Albury claims he was innocent. If he decides to clear his name then he may get to the truth.'

Jamie laughed. 'He can try, but I don't think he'll live very long.'

'Is that so?'

'Jamie, be careful,' Emma warned, but he rounded on her.

'Of what? He's not a copper and it's his word against ours. Listen, whatever your bloody name is, if Albury, or anyone else, including you, comes around stirring up trouble I don't think he'll be around long enough to draw his pension.'

'Are you threatening me?' I said lightly.

'Why don't you piss off?'

'With pleasure.'

I glanced at Joanne before heading back to the car. Obviously Andover had blackmailed Brookes and it had something to do with his daughter. Joanne Brookes, from what I had seen, was about as delicate as a thistle. There was defiance and hardness in her eyes, and a cruelty around her mouth that reminded me of Rowde. I was surprised that her father had paid Andover to keep silent about her, but then she had probably been his blue-eyed little girl.

I drove off with a last look at the manor house. I wondered if Jamie and Joanne Brookes had somehow discovered the true identity of Andover, killed him after he refused to say where the money was, buried the body and left me to take the rap. Then another more worrying fact dawned on me. By coming here and pretending I was a private detective I had alerted them about my own release. Would Jamie, Joanne, or their friends track down Alex Albury and attempt to eliminate him? If they did could I get to the truth before they killed me? Would my death silence Rowde and save my boys? That was possible, but my boys would grow up believing I really was a crook.

I turned into the Hare and Hounds public house about half a mile from where Joanne and Jamie lived and ordered myself a non-alcoholic lager. I opened a conversation with the barmaid and, half an hour later I had the information I needed, and was driving back to Portsmouth.

I caught the last ferry to the Island. My mind was teeming with ideas that led nowhere except to more questions that I didn't have answers for.

My head was throbbing when I stepped onto my houseboat and my chest felt tight with the knowledge that another day had passed that took me closer to my sons' fate, and I was nowhere nearer the truth.

I flicked on the light and froze. A wave of nausea washed over me. The room swam out of focus for a moment and I closed my eyes praying that what I saw on the floor wasn't there but was just a product of my overactive imagination. Slowly I opened my eyes. It was there all right. It was Westnam. He'd been strangled.

# CHAPTER 9

I averted my eyes and tried to catch my breath.
My heart was going like the clappers. God!
First Joe and now Westnam. Who next? I closed
my eyes trying to shut out the image of
Westnam's body, but all I could see was the limp
bodies of my sons lying before me, so I threw
them open again and hastily descended to the
kitchen where I poured myself a stiff whisky. I
tossed it back and felt the warmth slide down
my throat. I took some deep breaths, got myself
under control and returned to Westnam.

Rowde was responsible for this, I felt sure of

it. And yet Andover could have killed Westnam and planted him here to frame me again, but this time for murder. That made far more sense. Surely Rowde wouldn't want me behind bars when he thought he had the chance of getting three million pounds? Though it crossed my mind that Rowde could have killed Westnam as a reminder to me of what he would do to my boys if I didn't play ball. Well, I was playing, and part of Rowde's game, I guessed, required me to get rid of the body and erase all trace of it ever being on the houseboat. By killing Westnam, Rowde was implicating me further, building up more ammunition to manipulate me with. Yes, the more I thought about it the more convinced I became that this had Rowde's signature on it. I told myself that later I would go to the police and tell them the truth; I didn't have time for that now.

Moving a dead body requires an enormous amount of strength and in my pain-racked state it would require a superhuman effort. But I was strong and fit. Most of all I was desperate. I could do anything; move iron girders with my teeth if I had to in order to save my children. Not being seen was a different matter altogether. Scarlett seemed to have eyes in the back and sides of her head, a skill developed, I guessed, because of her mother's illness. And as her mother went walkabout at all hours of the day and night I couldn't be certain that the pair of them would be safely tucked up in bed.

It had started raining heavily. I was glad; it meant fewer people about to witness my activity. I consulted the tide timetable. The tide was just on the turn so I had no time to lose.

I stripped Westnam, noticing he had no papers on him, and bundled up his clothes. Then I found some lines and my sailing gloves and donning the gloves I tied one rope around Westnam's naked torso under his armpits and the other around his ankles. My hands were sweating and the perspiration was running down my face and back. I felt sick at what I was doing, but could only tell myself it was for my sons. I had no choice.

The wind was rising all the time, the last thing I wanted. I pulled on my sailing jacket and opened the patio doors. The wind and rain rushed in like Westnam's avenging spirit; lashing at my face.

I hauled Westnam's body along the floor, straining my ears for any sounds of life from Scarlett's houseboat. I thanked God for a dark, moonless night and although I cursed the wind and the rain, it kept all but the foolhardy, or guilty like me, indoors.

My yacht was moored up beneath the steps of the houseboat. Glancing to my right and left I hauled the body up as best I could, stifling my groans and praying that even the ones I couldn't stifle wouldn't be heard against the stormy night. Panting heavily and sweating profusely, I had Westnam almost in my arms leaning against me. I felt sick at the smell of death. Then, holding tight to the two ropes, I tipped his body over the edge head first. Slowly I let him slide down the edge of the houseboat easing the ropes until his head and upper torso touched the cockpit. My arms were almost pulled out of their sockets as I let down the rope. Then his crumpled, naked body lay in the yacht.

I locked the patio doors, pocketed the key, climbed on board my boat, and let off the lines. I started the engine, praying that no one would hear it, and turned into the wind. Thankfully as the tide rushed out it helped me.

It was dangerous but I knew the channel well. And it was deserted, not even the fishermen were foolish enough to go out in this. I wanted to get around the Foreland into Whitecliff Bay before I tossed Westnam overboard. Where he would end up I didn't know as long as it was away from me and my houseboat.

As I chugged into the tempestuous night I felt

sympathy for Westnam. What a bloody awful way to end your life! Andover had ruined Westnam's life as surely as he had ruined mine. I tried not to think of any relatives grieving for Westnam. I knew from Joe's reports that his ex wife was living in the States and they'd had no children.

The tide was beginning to push me to port when I wanted to go to starboard. I corrected my course. The waves splashed over the side of the small boat soaking both Westnam and me. Where he was he couldn't feel it and I was beyond caring about my own physical condition. My sailing jacket kept most of my body dry but my feet and legs were drenched in salt water, as were my face and hands. I could see one or two lights from the houses on the shore. This was far enough, any further and I'd be able to say hello to the container ships moored up for the night off Bembridge Ledge.

I grabbed Westnam's body. He was so heavy that I wondered if I'd be able to do it. My body screamed with pain, but with some superhuman effort I dredged up from God alone knew where, I hauled the poor sod over the side of the boat.

The splash his body made almost drowned me, as did the movement of the boat combined with the waves. It would have served me right if it had. I scurried into the cabin, found my spare anchor, and after wrapping Westnam's clothes around it I threw it in after him. Then I began my journey back. If I had thought going out was bad then returning was hell on earth. The tide wanted to take me back into the Solent.

I wasn't quite sure how I made it. Luck, God, whoever and whatever, and I was tying up alongside my houseboat, exhausted. I crashed down on the floor of the houseboat and fell asleep. When I awoke it was still dark, but a quick glance at my watch told me it wouldn't be long until dawn. I was cross with myself. How could I waste time sleeping when my sons' fate was in Rowde's hands? I shivered violently and tried to ease myself up. My arms felt as though they weighed more than the Clifton Suspension Bridge and my legs as though all the blood had been drained from them and the bone extracted leaving them wobbly, like one of those puppets in a children's television programme.

I was shattered but I hadn't finished yet. I had to scrub this room, then a hot shower, food and onward.

Four hours later I was changed and fed and there was, as far as I could see, no evidence that Westnam alive or dead had ever been here. I knew the drill at prison and that between 10am and 11am the visits booking line would be open. I

went out to a call box and asked to book a visit
with Ray. I'd forgotten that there was no visiting
on Thursdays and Fridays. Blast! I booked to see
him Saturday afternoon at 2pm, the earliest
possible time. Three days away and too close to
Rowde's deadline! But even though Ray was
incarcerated I knew that if I wanted information
on Jamie Redman, Joanne Brookes' partner, then
the prisoner network would give it to me.

I couldn't just sit around and kick my heels
until then though. I had to do something to find
Andover but the trail was getting colder by the
minute. There was only one person left for me
to try and that was Couldner's daughter, Lorraine
Proctor. I hurried out to the car where I'd left
Joe's reports containing the last address he had
for her. She lived just outside Chichester, not
far from the marina. It was quite a way to travel
if she wasn't in so I would telephone her from
the first call box I came to. Before I could climb
into the car a voice hailed me and I turned to see
the blonde goddess from Brading church
heading towards me.

She was dressed for hiking in shorts and
walking boots. Her honey blonde hair shone like
something out of a hair advertisement. She
looked the picture of such perfect health and
vitality that she made me feel positively ill. I

turned to see Scarlett at the door of her houseboat.

'What happened to you?' the blonde goddess said, a concerned expression on her beautiful face.

'I fell over. Too much to drink I expect,' I joked, impatient to be away. I heard Scarlett's door slam.

'You're Alex Albury. Percy Trentham told me after I described meeting you in Brading church. I'm Deeta.'

What else had Percy told her? That I was an ex con? If he had it didn't seem to bother her. I took the hand she proffered. Her grip was strong and dry. I didn't feel quite so much the embarrassed adolescent this time of meeting her, though I did silently wince at the memory of my ineptitude at our last encounter.

'How do you know Percy?' I was still suspicious of her.

'He has a metal detector. I see him on the beach sometimes. He's a mine of information about the Second World War.'

I recalled she had said she was writing a book about the Island at war. I didn't like to tell her that some of Percy's war stories were very dubious. She was the historian; she would check her sources.

She said, 'My grandfather lived here during the

early part of the war. Percy said you used to live in Bembridge House and that your grandfather built the folly there as an air raid shelter. It's a remarkable piece of architecture. Percy said your grandfather was a very important man in the war.'

'I don't think so. He died in a sailing accident in 1940. I shouldn't trust everything Percy tells you.'

'He likes to exaggerate. I looked your family up though. Did you know that you are descended from the Anglo-Saxons?'

'That might explain why I feel so old and tired sometimes.'

She laughed. Despite all my problems I couldn't prevent my loins from again responding to her beauty and her sensuality.

She said, 'Do you have any records that your father or grandfather left?'

'Sorry, no.' Any other time I would like to have talked to her. I would have flirted with her and I would certainly have invited her out for a drink. Now I was running out of time. She caught my agitation.

'I'm holding you up. Perhaps I will see you when you have more time.'

'I'd like that.' I watched her go with some sorrow. After almost four years without sex I meet a woman interested in me and I haven't got the time! That was sod's law for you all right.

I pulled up at a call box and punched in Lorraine Proctor's number. A lady answered who told me that Mrs Proctor would be back at two o'clock.

'Are you from the agency?' she asked.

'I beg your pardon.'

'The estate agency. Is it about the house?'

'Oh yes, that's right,' I said quickly, my mind racing. 'Who am I speaking to?'

'Mrs Ellis. I'm Mrs Proctor's cleaner.'

'Of course. Don't worry about any message, Mrs Ellis. It's not urgent. I'll call her later.'

Two o'clock, that gave me enough time to get to Chichester and find the house. Dear Mrs Ellis had given me my intro.

I rang Miles first though before setting out. 'What's the latest on Joe's death?'

'Random attack. Burglar after money.'

'What was he strangled with?'

'Something soft, a tie or scarf.'

Not bare hands then. Different to Westnam's strangulation, which could possibly indicate two killers: Rowde having killed Westnam and Andover, Joe.

'A burglar wearing a tie!' I said. 'Must be a pretty smart burglar.' For some reason Gus, immaculate in that suit and tie sitting in the kitchen, sprang to mind.

'Could have been a scarf, used to cover the lower part of the face so he couldn't be recognised.'

I gave him that one but I didn't go along with the random burglar theory.

'What about Sergeant Hammond, Clipton's sidekick?'

'He really did win the lottery.'

'Lucky him.'

I rang off and headed for the mainland. I reached Chichester just before one o'clock and parked in the multi-storey next to Waitrose. It was a bit of a long shot but if the house was up for sale then I guessed one of the more upmarket estate agents in the city would have the details on it.

I struck lucky at the third one I came to in East Street after collecting a number of housing details from the others, none of which matched Lorraine Proctor's address. Fifteen minutes later I left the estate agents clutching the details of Harbourside House and with an appointment to view, unaccompanied by the agent, which was a stroke of luck on a property worth almost a million pounds. But then I was due some luck and I had pushed hard for the appointment. I told them I had a meeting scheduled in London later that afternoon. I spun some yarn about being an IT entrepreneur with cash to burn in my pocket and the desperate need to find a house quickly for myself and family that was close to Chichester Harbour and with a mooring for my yacht. They all bought it. Goodness knows whether it would lead me to any information about Andover but I had to try. I had used the story about having an accident with a Mercedes on my return from the States to explain my battered and bruised face.

Lorraine Proctor opened the door to me. She was exquisitely dressed in camel-coloured trousers and a cream shirt that could only have come from a top designer. She, like the house, was a bit too polished and modern for me. It made me yearn for the informality of my houseboat. The thought rather surprised me. Before prison I would have wet myself in anticipation of living in a house like this, individually designed and commissioned by the owners with a glazed atrium, five bedrooms, a swimming pool and access to the harbour. Now I no longer aspired to it. In fact I wouldn't have wanted it as a gift.

'Mr Hardley?'

'Yes.' I'd used my mother's maiden name. 'It's very good of you to see me at such short notice.'

'Not at all. Where would you like to start?'

'Downstairs, I think.'

She hadn't recognised me behind the bruises or the white hair. I had wondered if she might. Neither had she shown any shock at my battered face, nor asked me questions about it, I guessed the agent had called her to explain.

After a tour of the hall, sitting room, kitchen and breakfast room we stepped into the study. From here I could look out across the garden to the upper reaches of Chichester Harbour and to the South Downs beyond. It was beautiful. A sailor's paradise with a Bavaria 42 yacht moored at the bottom of the garden.

'It's perfect,' I said, thinking more of the yacht and location than the house. On the tour we'd chatted about how long she'd lived here: six years. What her husband did for a living: consultant surgeon. I was wondering how to bring up the subject of her father and Andover. Waiting for inspiration I gazed at photographs of racing yachts on the walls. 'You sail?' I asked.

'When I can, with my husband. He also races yachts.'

'You'll miss living here.'

'Not really, we're moving to Hayling Island. We've bought a house with a mooring that gives us direct access into Langstone Harbour and the Solent. It takes quite a while to sail up through Chichester Harbour until you reach the Solent.

It's an art deco house that needs some work. I shall enjoy that.'

'Is interior design your business? I must say you have immaculate taste.'

Whatever she answered it by-passed me. Suddenly I was staring at a large photograph of a beautiful yacht with a full spinnaker and a hardworking crew racing in the Solent. Where had I seen the name on the spinnaker before? Spires. Of course it had been on the notepad in Gus's hall, beside the pilot's licence. I took a step nearer and eagerly scanned the other photographs. There was one of the crew in harbour; the skipper was holding a magnum of champagne to celebrate their victory.

'Is this your husband?' I asked pointing to a tall blonde man beside the older man holding the champagne.

'Yes, and that's my father beside him. He was killed in a car accident the summer after this photograph was taken.'

The year before my arrest. 'Who's this?' I asked pointing to one of the crew. I knew who it was: Gus Newberry. I wanted to know if she did.

'Probably someone who worked for my father.'

I didn't have a clue where Gus worked or what connection he had with Sidney Couldner, only that there was a connection. It didn't necessarily mean anything. It could just be a coincidence. Yet it niggled me.

I raced through the rest of the house with only a fraction of my mind on it. After a hasty goodbye I drove around to Chichester marina and parked the car. Opening the boot I scrabbled through my press cuttings file until I found the one I wanted. I knew I'd seen the name Spires somewhere other than on Gus's notepad. They had been Manover Plastics accountants; there was a reference to them in one of the articles on Clive Westnam. Why hadn't I seen the connection before? Because it had needed the photograph and the notepad to link it. Was there a connection with Brookes? I wouldn't mind betting so.

With my heart hammering against my ribs fit to bust I used the pay phone in the marina café and called Spires. Some minutes later I had the information I needed. Gus was their senior partner, specialising in corporate finance. I rang off and headed for Petersfield.

# CHAPTER 10

'Alex! What's happened to you?' Vanessa greeted me with a horror-stricken expression.

'This?' I fingered my bruised face. 'An accident.' She looked as though she didn't believe me, but that was the least of my problems.

It was after school hours and yet the house was as quiet as the grave. I had wondered on my drive across country to Petersfield if I would see my sons but they couldn't be here. I was disappointed. Then Vanessa tossed an anxious glance over her shoulder and I knew I was wrong.

My heart leapt into my throat. Before I realised it I had pushed past her and was tearing down the hall, all thoughts of Gus vanishing from my mind.

I drew up on the threshold of the kitchen. I thought I was going to pass out at the sight of them in school uniform sitting at the table, their heads bent over their homework. I was sure my heart had stopped beating. I stood perfectly still afraid that I might spoil the moment by bursting into tears, something I hadn't done since I had fallen off the roof of Grandad's folly and broken my arm. My crying in prison had been inside me, churning my gut until the pain had become almost unbearable, sucking the breath from my lungs.

Then they both looked up. My heart started beating again; it was as if someone had put one of those resuscitating machines on it and had kick-started it into life. I took a breath. I wanted to wrap my arms around them, to hold them tight and never let them go. I wanted to save them from bastards like Rowde. But I couldn't even move. Vanessa stepped in front of me.

'You can finish your homework upstairs.'

Her words brought me out of my emotional rigor. Gently I pushed her aside. 'Hello.' I sounded like someone with laryngitis. I tried to smile, maybe I did. I hoped I didn't look like the ventriloquist's dummy from *Dead of Night*.

David glanced at his mother. It angered me.

'You don't need permission to speak to your father,' I said more harshly than I intended.

'Are you my dad?' Philip said, excitedly and slightly in awe.

How could he have forgotten me so quickly? He had been almost eight when I had gone inside; I had been seven when my father had died of a heart attack. I hadn't forgotten the gentle quiet man who had read to me and taught me how to sail, so why had Philip forgotten me? Perhaps the hair had fooled him, or possibly my bruised face. Perhaps Vanessa and Gus had banished all photographs of me from the house. I glared at her. She flinched and I wanted to crow because I had hurt her. Suddenly I felt extremely sad.

I smiled again, more naturally I hoped this time. 'Yes. Don't you remember me?' I told myself a child's memory was very short. And I had not allowed them to send me a card or letter whilst I had been in prison. Vanessa had persuaded me it was for the best, though I hadn't need much persuasion.

'Your hair's white,' David said.

'Prison did that to me.'

Vanessa winced. The boys didn't bat an eyelid. I parked myself at the top of the table with

David on my right and Philip on my left. It took all my powers of self-control not to scoop them up in my arms and hold them so tight that I might be in danger of suffocating them. My heart was breaking. I hoped they couldn't see it.

'What's prison like?' Philip wriggled, impatient to be let loose. He had always been the more active child. Many a time he and I had kicked a ball around the park, while David had preferred to have his nose buried in a book. I dug my nails into the palm of my hands underneath the table so hard that I wondered if I had drawn blood.

'Philip, your father doesn't want to talk about it. Now upstairs –'

'It's horrible and smelly and lonely.'

'Did you meet loads of crooks?'

David scoffed. 'Of course he did. Why else do you think they're in prison.'

'Dad's not a crook.' Philip declared hotly.

I felt the tears spring to my eyes. It took a supreme effort of will to hold them back. I gripped the top of the table as if it was going to collapse if I didn't hold onto it, when in reality it was me that was in danger of collapsing.

'You're not a crook, are you, Dad?'

'No, Philip, I'm not.' I held the clear, innocent blue eyes that gazed at me.

David, now fourteen, looked as though he wasn't sure whether or not to believe me, but I saw something in his serious brown eyes that wanted me to be telling the truth.

I addressed them both. 'I was sent to prison for something I didn't do and now I have to prove I'm innocent.'

'Like in that film with Harrison Ford?' David eyed me curiously.

I must have looked puzzled because he explained as if talking to a rather stupid child, '*The Fugitive*. He's trying to find the one-armed man who killed his wife.'

'Aren't you a little young to have seen that?'

'Nah, we've all seen it, except Philip; he's still a baby.'

'I'm not. I'm nearly as old as you.'

'You're two years younger,' David said haughtily.

Oh my God, how I had missed this, the endless sparring between them, at one time friends, next fighting on the living room floor. Andover had deprived me of this. He would be punished. I was in for the kill now.

'Philip, David, upstairs at once and take your homework. Your father and I need to talk.'

David rolled his eyes but scooped up his textbooks. I watched the boys slide off their chairs. At the door David hesitated.

'You will find out who really did it, won't you, Dad?'

'I will.'

'And you'll come back and play with us like you used to?'

I nodded. I was beyond speech. He remembered.

'That's what I told them at school.'

'David,' I called him back, finding my voice. 'What did you tell them?'

'That you were going after the man who put that stuff on your computer.'

'You think someone did.'

'Of course. Anyone can hack into computers. You can make them say what you want and people believe it because they think computers can't lie. It's easy.'

'Room now,' came Vanessa's stern command.

David grinned. I smiled back and he ran off.

'Alex –'

'They're great; they're so grown up. They're so…' My voice faltered. I rose and turned away from her. I could hear them scuffling about upstairs, a toilet flushed and a door banged. When I had myself under control Vanessa had a whisky in front of me but I shook my head.

'I'm driving. Coffee would be good though; help keep me awake.'

She turned away and flicked the switch on the kettle. I was glad that Gus hadn't been here. It had given me the chance to be with my sons. I felt sick to the pit of my stomach at the thought of what Rowde threatened to do to them. If Gus had any part to play in framing me then I'd kill the bastard. But how could he have? And why? It wasn't possible and yet there was that pilot's licence, the fact that he knew Couldner, and that he worked for Spires: Clive Westnam's accountants. I told myself that knowing two out of the three victims wasn't proof that Gus had any connection with Andover. And yet…

'When will Gus be in?' I asked, wondering if Vanessa would notice the hardness in my voice.

'Monday evening, if all goes well with the deal.'

'What?' I shouted. I hadn't expected this. It spoilt all my plans.

She gazed at me surprised. 'He's in Guernsey, on business.'

Guernsey! My heart sank. How long would it take me to get there, get some answers from Gus, and then fly back again? A day at least and I didn't have a day to spare. I wouldn't be able to get a flight until tomorrow, Friday, *if* I was lucky. Maybe not until Saturday. There was one good thing though; at least I didn't need a passport to get to Guernsey. It could have been worse; it could have been Hong Kong!

'What kind of business?' I forced myself to keep calm. If I couldn't get to Gus until tomorrow, then I could at least get some answers to my questions from Vanessa now.

'I don't know. Something to do with one of his clients, I expect.'

'Who is he seeing in Guernsey?'

'Alex, what is this?'

'Just humour me.' I tried to keep a lid on my impatience.

'Fosters, they're private bankers based just outside St Peter Port. I think there's a big deal going down with some property developers. I don't understand it and I don't ask.'

I could hear David and Philip talking and laughing, not a lot of homework was being done. 'When did you meet Gus?' I asked steadily.

A faint flush spread up her neck. The kettle boiled and flicked itself off. Vanessa made no attempt to make me a coffee. She sat down, looked at her hands and then up at me with a defiant gleam in her eyes. I could see that she had come to a decision. I wasn't sure that I wanted to hear this, but I had asked for it. Somehow I knew it was going to be painful.

'We first met when I was a student at Manchester University. I was twenty. Gus was twenty eight.'

I kept my eyes on her and my expression blank, but my brain was whirring around like a demented dervish. She'd never said. She'd never spoken of Gus Newberry before. I didn't even know he had existed until Miles had told me she had married him. When Vanessa had asked for a divorce she had said it was because she had wanted to make a new life for herself and the boys. Oh, she'd done that all right.

'He was attending a conference in a nearby hotel. We met in a pub by the canal, not far from China Town and we hit it off immediately. I thought him very sophisticated. Even when he returned to London he used to call me. At weekends he'd come to Manchester, or I'd go up to London. After six months we got engaged.'

'Why didn't you tell me this before?' I felt betrayed.

'It wasn't important. Gus and I had finished long before I met you.'

'How long?' I asked curtly, wondering if I had been taken up on the rebound, a thought I didn't much care for. No one likes to be thought of as second best.

'Five years.'

'Why did you break up?'

She ran a hand through her hair. 'Alex, is this necessary?' She must have seen from my expression that it was because she added, 'You've grown hard.' She rose and began to pace the floor.

'Funny, you wouldn't think prison would do that to a man, would you?'

'There's no need to be sarcastic. If you must know we broke up because he was very ambitious. He was offered a promotion, which meant working in the States. He wanted me to leave university and go with him. I said no. I wanted a career too. We kept in touch for quite a while then it fizzled out. I met you.'

'So when did you see him again? I take it that it was whilst we were still married.' I couldn't keep the bitterness from my voice.

She met my gaze directly. There was no hint of regret or shame in her expression.

'I met him by chance,' she said. 'We were on the Isle of Wight. I saw him at the airfield. He has a private pilot's licence and flew into Bembridge one day when you'd taken the boys out sailing. I'd gone for a walk.'

I felt a tightening in my chest. It wasn't only jealousy. Slowly the pieces were fitting together. Could Gus *be* Andover?

'When was this?' I asked.

Her face flushed deeper red betraying what I'd already guessed: she'd had an affair with him whilst we'd still been married. It hurt. Even my marriage wasn't what it had seemed.

'Three years before your arrest. Alex, I'm sorry. Nothing happened between us until… until…'

'I was arrested.'

Jesus! Gus *was* Andover. Vanessa had just given me his motive. Incredible as it seemed he had stitched me up in order to steal my wife and children. Had Vanessa told him she couldn't leave me? Perhaps Gus couldn't take rejection. A clever bastard like him could have worked out a way to ruin me and then provided the shoulder for Vanessa to cry on. He'd seen her through the tough times; even convincing her I was innocent. Well, he should know.

I leapt up. I wanted to beat Gus Newberry until he begged for forgiveness for destroying me. She hurried after me to the door. At it I turned and said:

'Did Gus know when I was being released?'

'Yes. He took the call from Miles.'

'Where was he the day I came out?'

'At work. For goodness sake, Alex, what is all this?'

I was already at the car. 'Take care, Vanessa, and please look after our sons. I'll be back as soon as I can.'

'Where are you going?'

To Guernsey. Where else? I didn't tell her that.

# CHAPTER 11

I found a travel agency in Petersfield and booked my flight for 10.55am the next morning, Friday, from Southampton to Guernsey.

It was just after seven when I disembarked at Fishbourne. Impatient though I was to get some answers from Gus there was nothing I could do except wait for tomorrow. Then another thought struck me: would Vanessa warn Gus? She didn't know I was going to Guernsey but she might tell him that she had confessed to the affair.

Gus's words came back to me, *'You're dealing with a very clever man. I suspect he knows your every move before you've even made it.'* I hoped he didn't know this one. I wanted to surprise the bastard.

My head was pounding and my back was still aching from the beating Rowde's henchman had given me. I was tired. I wanted to lay down and sleep for a year. A car tooted at me as I veered dangerously over the white line onto the other side of the road at the bend towards St Helen's. I jerked the steering wheel back and forced myself to concentrate. It wasn't easy.

Surely if I told Gus about Rowde's threat to my boys he'd hand over the money? He had to. I couldn't imagine him letting any harm come to David and Philip because if it did it would destroy his relationship with Vanessa. That cheered me. Gus hadn't counted on Rowde. I might actually end up being grateful to Rowde, strange though it might seem.

As I pulled into the narrow lay-by opposite my houseboat I glimpsed a figure by the door and with a jolt recognised it was Deeta. I wasn't sure whether to be pleased or irritated. It was late. I wanted to ease my aching body before my trip to Guernsey tomorrow, but now I'd have to invite her in and make small talk. That's what my brain said, other parts of my body were telling me something quite different and small talk didn't feature in it. Whether I would have the energy for those more amorous and athletic inclinations was a different matter though.

She turned to face me. I expected a smile, but what I got was an expression out of a Hammer horror movie that curdled my blood. Her skin was almost opaque with terror and her blue eyes wide and alarmed. I rushed towards her stifling a groan that could have been even louder than the one I'd uttered climbing out of the car. What now for God's sake! Had Rowde planted more dead bodies on my houseboat?

She pointed at my open door. I guessed I was pale by now. With a quickening heartbeat, that would have had a heart surgeon salivating, I tentatively pushed open the door and stepped inside. Thank God. No body, only chaos. I let out a long, slow sigh of relief. I had been burgled.

I quickly ran my eye around the room; cushions were strewn on the floor, the cupboards opened and their contents tossed around. I guessed it was the same down below but didn't get a chance to find out as Deeta came up behind me.

'Who could have done such a terrible thing?' she cried aghast.

Rowde most probably. One of his little warnings, like Westnam's body. Yet, as my eyes surveyed the mess I knew that whoever had done this had been searching for something rather than simply being destructive, as Rowde would have been. Someone who'd had to act very quickly. I'd seen enough cells turned over to spot the signs.

Deeta seemed really shaken. I lifted the cushion onto the seat. 'Sit down. You need a drink.'

'I should be saying that to you.'

I was surprised to see how distressed she was. It was as if her home had been violated not mine.

'We both need a drink,' I said gently, going below to fetch one. It gave me a chance to see where else my intruder had left his mark. The galley wasn't too bad; at least the crockery was still in the cupboards. I found a bottle of red wine and two glasses and dived into my bedroom before returning to the upper deck.

My clothes were strewn about the floor. I remembered my mother's jewellery. It was all there, still in the box file, in its plastic bag: her wedding and engagement ring, a couple of brooches, a silver locket and a gold bracelet. The photographs had been tossed on the floor along with the diaries.

'Has anything been taken?'

I swung round to find Deeta standing in the

doorway. Her tight jeans and even tighter T-shirt showed off her figure to perfection. My heart began to beat faster this time with excitement and longing rather than fear.

'Not that I can see,' I said. This was one thing I couldn't lay at Gus's door. Unless he had flown back in a private plane as soon as Vanessa had telephoned him after my visit, landing at Bembridge airfield... stop being so bloody stupid, I scolded myself.

I made to move back upstairs when Deeta stepped further into the bedroom. I cleared my throat and tried to look relaxed. I wasn't sure if I succeeded.

'These photographs, they're of you as a child.'

Before I could stop her she had picked up a handful of photographs and was sitting on the bed. OK, I thought, might as well join her. I opened the bottle and poured her a glass.

She took a sip and gave me a look that was both assessing and admiring, but maybe I just wanted it to be so. I could hardly breathe from being so close to her. I could smell her light scent. My hands ached to touch a woman, my arms to embrace one...

'Are you always this calm in a crisis?'

If only she knew. 'Not always.' I felt an overwhelming desire to confide. It would be such a relief just to be able to talk to someone about what was happening to me, but it would also put that person in danger. I couldn't do it. Besides, in prison, I had learnt the hard way, never to confide in anyone, it only led to trouble.

'How come you found this?' I asked, sweeping an arm to take in the destruction.

'I was passing and thought that maybe you had returned.' She dashed a glance at me and I felt flattered by it. 'I saw your door was open.' She was regaining some of her colour. 'What were they after?'

I shrugged and sipped my wine. Money? The code to the Swiss bank account where my millions were stashed away?

'Aren't you going to call the police?' She frowned, puzzled.

'Why? They won't be able to do anything and they certainly won't catch whoever did it.'

'What about the insurance?'

'Not worth it,' I dismissed.

This break-in was the least of my worries. But sitting here with her, drinking wine, the tension began to ease a little. Oh, my anxiety was still burrowing away inside my gut, and I was impatient for action but, I kept telling myself, there was nothing I could do until tomorrow. Her slender hands were flicking through the photographs.

'What happened to you, Alex?' she asked suddenly. 'Percy says you went to prison for stealing money, is it true?'

'No.' I felt the involuntary stiffening of my body. She noticed it.

'I believe you.'

'Why?'

'You look honest.'

I laughed. 'I wish you'd been on the jury. No, I'm not making fun of you, Deeta,' I added hastily, seeing her puzzled and slightly dejected look. 'Someone framed me.'

'Tell me about it.' She looked at me over the edge of her wine glass.

I'd rather kiss you, I thought. 'I'd only bore you.'

'I don't think you'd do that, Alex.'

My heart went into overdrive. I wanted so much to make love to her and yet I was half scared to death to even try. It had been such a long time.

She picked up the photograph of me with the telescope. 'It must have been magical growing up in a place like this and with such a beautiful, caring mother. You can see she loves you by the look in her eyes and the way she has her arm around you.'

'I know.' My voice faltered for a moment.

'Did she ever talk about the old days? About her father?'

'Teddy Hardley?' I shook my head. 'Not much. He died when she was quite young.'

'And he never left any letters, or a diary?'

'No. Why the interest?'

'I'm an historian, remember.' She gazed steadily at me with those big blue eyes. My heart was melting and my loins were on fire with desire.

'I am always interested in the past,' she said.

'It's only the present that matters to me.' I didn't want her to leave. She would be a distraction for me, and a pleasant one at that. That sounded callous. I didn't mean it to be. Or did I? For one night she might help me to forget about the past and the future. It was selfish of me, but I was sure it was what she also wanted. What she saw in me I didn't know, and I didn't want to ask.

I placed my glass on the table. I could smell her perfume; feel her soft breath near my face. I leaned over and kissed her. Her lips were so soft and willing against mine. My whole body was on fire. I put my arms around her and she responded so eagerly that it almost scared me off; her tongue was seeking mine, her slender body pressing against me. I could feel her softness. For some reason Scarlett's voluptuous figure popped into my mind. But I hastily banished the thought of her and did what any man would have done in the circumstances, I made love to Deeta, twice. The first time I'm ashamed to admit was a purely selfish act on my part. The second time, I hoped she got just as much pleasure from it as me. I didn't hear her complaining.

It was early morning when I woke.

'I didn't mean to disturb you,' she said gently, pulling on her jeans.

I lay back with my hands behind my head and watched her dress. For a moment I forgot that I was going to Guernsey. But only for a moment. I glanced at my watch. It was just after 6am. I pulled myself up.

'Do you want a coffee or something to eat?'

'No. I have to go.' She leaned across the bed and kissed me. It was enough to stir me into action again. She pulled away laughing. 'Thank you for a lovely night.'

It should have been me thanking her. I watched her walk away then grabbed a coffee, and some breakfast, showered, changed, and locked up the houseboat. Outside I hesitated before knocking on Scarlett's door. There was no answer, but I knew she was in. I could hear the radio playing.

I headed for the Red Funnel service from Cowes to Southampton. The flight to Guernsey was delayed. They didn't say why. It was 11.30am when I stepped onto the aeroplane. It landed just over an hour later.

I hailed a taxi to take me to St Peter Port. I didn't have time to look at the blue rippling waters of the harbour, or the quaint town with its pretty colour-washed houses climbing the hill on my left. We followed the harbour round, keeping it on our right until, on the outskirts of the old town, we came to the new development of steel and glass: the glitzy offices of the financiers who had succeeded the Germans, the Guernsey cows and the tomatoes.

The receptionist told me that Mr Newberry was in a meeting.

'I have to see him urgently,' I insisted. 'I have some bad news about his wife and sons. There's been an accident.'

The girl looked horrified. My bruised face convinced her I was telling the truth. She quickly made to telephone him when I stilled her. I didn't want Gus running out the back way.

'I think it's best if I go along there and tell him, rather than confront him here in reception, don't you?'

She didn't seem to be sure but I put on my most sympathetic face and finally she said,

'Meeting room six on the top floor. The lift is behind you, sir.'

I hadn't thought through what I would say, just that I'd get him by the throat and beat the truth out of him if I had too. The vision of at least fifteen years behind bars for the murder of Westnam, with bullies like Rowde, not to mention my children's safety, was enough to make me desperate.

I scanned the numbers on the meeting room doors in the silence of the air-conditioned corridor, my heart beating rapidly, my palms sweating, until I was in front of number six. Ignoring the 'engaged' sign I thrust open the door and all eight faces of the men sitting, jacketless, around a long boardroom table, scattered with papers and bottles of Perrier, looked up at me. Gus was sitting directly opposite where I was standing. His was the only expression I noted and that barely as I swiftly crossed the carpeted room. Within an instant I had him by the throat, pinned up against the wall.

'Where is it, you bastard?' I roared. I was only vaguely conscious of movement behind me but nobody remonstrated with me. Gus croaked something but I wasn't listening, I was too busy banging his head against the wall.

'Where's the fucking money?' I screeched. His face was red; his eyes bulging like a bullfrog. He was struggling to speak. He was choking. I let him go and his body slumped to the floor. I balled my fist and held it back ready to smash it into his face when it was grabbed. I was spun round and a fist smashed into *my* face. My head rocked back and I staggered against the wall. The fist came up again but this time I heard Gus shout, 'Leave him.'

My blurred vision began to clear and I saw a burly security guard wearing a uniform that the SS would have been proud of. Reluctantly he stepped back, a disappointed expression on his face. Gus reached out a hand. The smug bastard, I thought, trying to struggle up without his assistance.

The other men were standing by the door muttering and looking grim. I stumbled, reached for the corner of the table for support and shook my head as the room swam out of focus, then wish I hadn't as pain shot through it. I sat down with a groan, putting my head in my hands. When I looked up, the room was empty except for Gus and there was glass of water in front of me.

'Drink it,' he commanded.

I tried to glare at him but it hurt my head too much. Ignoring the drink I rubbed a hand against my lip and tasted the blood. Pulling out a handkerchief I wiped my mouth. Gus was now sitting on my right. He looked drained, but I bet he was a picture of health compared to me.

'Where's the money, Gus? Or should I say Andover?' I snapped. Gus looked surprised. He wasn't fooling me. 'You lied about how long you had known Vanessa. You were having an affair with her. You wanted to steal her from me and the only way you thought you could do that was to disgrace me.'

I could feel my anger rising again, yet something in Gus's expression told me I was wrong. His shock and surprise seemed genuine. I had to be right. My sons' future depended on it.

I continued. 'You can fly an aeroplane, you know all about computers and you have a connection with two of the victims. Westnam was chief executive of Manover Plastics and your firm were his accountants. Spires sponsored the Beckenham Challenge Cup and Couldner raced in that. Spires is plastered all over the spinnaker and you're in a photograph alongside Couldner.'

'And Brookes?'

'They'll be a connection.'

'Alex, this is crazy.'

'No.' I spat. 'Crazy is what you did to me. You knew a secret about each man, one worth blackmailing for. Perhaps Westnam's accounts weren't quite legit; perhaps Brookes had inflated the profits for the takeover by Sunglow, and Couldner's secret could be something you learned whilst drinking with him in the yacht club.'

'You've got this all wrong. Where does the aeroplane come in?'

I told him about the incident on the day of my release.

I studied him carefully. I knew he was clever. 'There's no use in denying it any longer, Gus. I met some very nasty men in prison. One of them called Rowde is now free and he wants the money I don't have. In return for which he says he won't harm my sons.'

Gus turned pale. 'You're not serious?'

Looking at him, I began to have doubts. His terror was no act; no one went that pale on demand. I said nothing.

He reached for a bottle of water, poured himself a glass and drank it down in one go. He was visibly shaken and looked physically ill. Serve him bloody well right I thought. It was about time something ruffled his oh-so-perfect fucking life. But that was stupid because nothing mattered except my children.

Gus was recovering. He was not the impetuous type. Instead he had been gathering his thoughts and his composure. Behind his slow deliberate manner I could see a brain that could operate at the speed of lightning. He said, 'Does Vanessa know about this?'

'Of course she doesn't.' I rubbed a hand across my eyes. I felt exhausted.

'And the police? Have you been to the police?'

'Get real! How can I tell the police? They'd never believe me and Rowde would know the minute I did.'

'What are you going to do?'

I pulled myself up. '*You're* going to tell me where the money is and then *I'm* going to get it and give it to Rowde.'

He stared at me as if I'd grown two heads. 'I don't know where the money is.'

'Wrong answer, Gus.'

'You still think that I'm Andover?' he cried incredulously.

I remained silent but kept my eyes on him. Surely it was him? It had to be.

'You must believe me for the sake of your sons and Vanessa, I am not Andover. I admit I saw her when you were still married to her and I'm sorry for that. I also admit that I never stopped loving her from the moment I met her years ago when she was at university. But I am not Andover and I didn't frame you.'

Either he was telling the truth or he was a very good actor. But would I know the truth if it was staring me in the face?

'Go to the police, Alex. You have to for the boys' sake.'

I hesitated, holding his stare. I could see he was in earnest. I had got it wrong. My body slumped. What remaining energy I had drained from me. My quest to find Andover and save my sons seemed hopeless.

'Rowde might get to them first. He knows where they are and he has probably seen me make a dash for the airport. He may think I've already run away with the money.'

'Then we need to act fast. Come on.' Gus had the door open and was striding down the corridor before I could blink. I scrambled after him. The security guard eyed us curiously.

'Are you OK, Mr Newberry?'

'Get me a car, Johnson, and now. Ask someone to pack my things and check me out of my hotel. They can bring my luggage to the airport. Get two seats on the first flight out of here and if there isn't one, hire me a private plane. Alex, did you check in anywhere?'

'No, I came straight here. I haven't even got an overnight bag,' I stammered, stunned by his swift course of action.

He mumbled something to the receptionist who looked very upset and then we hovered outside until a car drew up about a minute later and Gus urged me to climb inside.

'If we can get back to England before Rowde gets to Vanessa and the boys, I'll get them out of the country and make sure they're safe. I'll call Vanessa.'

I watched him stab at his mobile phone, his fingers impatiently tapping against the side of his leg as he waited for an answer.

'Damn, her mobile's not switched on. I'll try the school.'

I felt my stomach muscles go into spasm. I was beginning to get nervous. I had a terrible premonition that we were already too late and that instead of making love to a beautiful woman, and then haring here like a mad man, I should have been taking my boys and Vanessa away from that school and into hiding, just as Gus now proposed. I couldn't even get that right. I heard Gus ask for Mrs Newberry.

'When?'

He cursed and called the house, throwing me the look of a man who'd just seen his winning lottery ticket go up in flames. I knew what he was going to say even before he said it. He left a curt message for Vanessa to call him urgently as soon as she got in. I didn't think she was going to pick that message up, just yet.

We kicked our heels round the airport for a while. Whoever the security guard had instructed, she had managed to get us both on the 16.10 flight to Southampton. Soon we were in my car heading for Petersfield. Neither of us spoke.

The house was empty. You could tell that as soon as you stepped inside. There was a note on the kitchen table. Gus read it, took a deep breath and fetched two glasses of whisky. He put one down in front of me.

'They've gone?' I asked, already knowing the answer to my question.

Gus nodded and tossed back his drink.

I said, 'Do you know what the saddest words in the English language are? Too late.'

'What do we do now?' Gus sat down opposite me. He was deathly pale.

'We wait for Rowde to call.'

'Shouldn't we go to the police?' Gus's cool composure had gone the way of the dodo. His tie was awry, his jacket off, sweat patches showed under his arms and his hair was all over the place.

I began to pace the room. 'No. Rowde won't hurt them if he thinks he's got a chance of getting the three million. So I'll give it to him.'

'You have it?'

'No, but Rowde doesn't know that.' Suddenly it was quite clear what I had to do. 'I'll say that it's in a Swiss bank account and that I have to go in person to withdraw it. He can come with me.'

'Will he believe you?'

I didn't blame Gus for looking sceptical 'I'll make sure he does. It might be a good idea if you lie low for a while. Get away from here and stay away until I tell you it's OK.'

'I can't do that.'

'Rowde will keep hold of Vanessa and my sons, knowing that I'll do anything to protect them, but you took them from me so you are expendable. In Rowde's reckoning I hate you and he won't hesitate to kill you, or have you killed. He's a cruel bastard. Why they ever let him out I don't know, but then that's the system for you.'

What colour was left in Gus's face drained away. I thought he was going to faint. In barely a whisper he said, 'I'll stay at –'

'I don't want to know, that way I can't tell. I'll call you and let you know as soon as Rowde makes contact.'

I drove back to Portsmouth and caught the Wight Link ferry to the Island. By the time I reached my houseboat it was late. My eyelids were scratching my eyes. I was so damned tired. I had only just put my key in the lock when a soft voice hailed me. I was surprised to see Scarlett step out of the shadows.

'What is it?' I began irritably. I didn't have time to think about her mother or look for her if she had gone missing again. Then something in Scarlett's expression made my heart leap into my throat. I knew it meant trouble, and for me. I could see it. I could smell it.

'It's that woman, the blonde one who was on your houseboat,' Scarlett began.

Deeta. I felt cold and full of dread.

'She's dead. She's been murdered.'

## Chapter 12

Deeta dead. I couldn't believe it. It was impossible. I must have said as much aloud because Scarlett picked up on it:

'It's true. Percy found her on the beach. He was out with his metal detector. He's being treated for shock.'

I bet, and then he'll live off the tale for the next ten years. But that was unkind, and probably untrue. God, what a mess! Poor Deeta. 'How?' I asked abruptly.

'I don't know.'

Who could have killed her? Why? My mind

raced as I saw Scarlett scan the wrecked interior of my houseboat. When her eyes came back to rest upon me they looked puzzled and a little hurt. I felt a stab of guilt as though I had betrayed her. It was ridiculous. Scarlett meant nothing to me.

'I saw her leaving here the morning she was killed,' she said.

'I didn't kill her.'

'I know. I watched you leave about half an hour after she did. You climbed into your car and drove off in the opposite direction.'

'I could have doubled back.'

'You could have, but you didn't.'

She said it so confidently and dismissively that I could have hugged her.

'When did Percy find her?' A terrible thought had entered my brain and blotted out everything else. How long was it after she had left me and after we had made love?

'This morning, just before seven. He came running up the lane to the hotel. I don't know why he didn't call the police before he reached there, but that could be something to do with the shock.'

My heart sank. Deeta had left me just before six-thirty. She must have decided to walk around the beach back to the hotel and someone had followed her. When they got Deeta on that mortuary slab they'd discover that she'd had sex before she was killed. They'd test for DNA. I was a criminal. I was on the national database. They'd have a match. How long before they came looking for me? How long before Westnam's body was washed up on the shore? How long before they connected these deaths with me? Oh, this was good. This was a far better frame up than before. This time I would go down for murder.

'Will you tell the police about Deeta being on my houseboat?' I asked anxiously.

She held my gaze. There was still that hostility in her eyes but this time I thought it was tinged with a world-weary sadness. 'Why should I?'

I probably had a couple of days at the most before the police connected me with Deeta's death. I couldn't go into hiding because Rowde had to find me. I just hoped he would before the police.

After Scarlett had gone I lay down. I didn't even contemplate sleeping. My heart was heavy with the sadness of Deeta's death. Only last night we had lain here together. I could still smell the scent of her firm young body. I could hear her laugh and her gentle questioning about my childhood and family. It had felt so good to talk to someone.

I had nearly told her about Rowde, but at the final moment remained silent. I had seen the surprise and shock in her eyes when she'd seen the bruises on my torso that had come courtesy of Rowde's henchman, and the scars that Rowde and my other tormenters in prison had inflicted on me.

Poor Deeta. She had been so alive, so vibrant. How could she no longer exist? Next it would be Rowde's turn to kill. My sons and ex wife would die. Enough. I couldn't let anything happen to them. I would have to kill Rowde, but first I needed to know where they were.

I didn't intend to sleep but fatigue finally overcame anxiety and I woke to the sound of the birds. It was just on five o'clock, and it was Saturday. I had three days before Rowde carried out his threat.

There was no point going back to sleep. I couldn't even if I wanted to. If Gus wasn't Andover then I had to start again. And I was going to start with that aeroplane. Someone at the airfield might know who the pilot was, or perhaps had recognised the aeroplane. I should have done this earlier but events had swept me in a different direction.

This afternoon I was due at Camp Hill Prison to see Ray. My idea that Spires had linked the three businessmen had proven to be false; I was back to Emma Brookes, her daughter Joanne and partner, Jamie Redman. The airfield and Ray were my last hopes and I wasn't optimistic about either.

There was no sign of life in Scarlett's houseboat as I passed it. There was also no sign of Rowde. The bastard was making me sweat. At a call box in the village I telephoned to Gus on his mobile. He hadn't heard from Vanessa. He had interrogated the home telephone remotely, from wherever he had gone to ground. There was no message. He sounded dreadful, but assured me that he was safe.

It was too early yet to go to the airfield so I decided to walk along the shore. It was a clear, crisp morning with a slight breeze that rippled the sea onto the sand. I would have enjoyed it if my mind hadn't been so disturbed by concerns for Vanessa and the boys.

I came to where Deeta's body had been found. It was just below the footpath that led up to Swains Road, a select area of Bembridge village. The blue and white police tape flapped in the wind. I stood for a moment in the silence of the early morning feeling an ache inside me as I recalled her beauty. She had paid a terrible price for the sake of framing me. I couldn't believe Rowde had killed her, not that he wasn't capable of it, he was, but if he had known that I cared for Deeta, he would have threatened me with her life, just as he was doing with my sons and Vanessa. No, the man who had killed Deeta was the same man who had humiliated and ruined me: Andover. He was still persecuting me and Deeta had been his instrument. I had to get to him before anyone else suffered the same fate.

I found myself climbing the coastal path and heading through the somnolent holiday camps and towards the airfield. There was a man tinkering with a small aeroplane in one of the hangars. He looked vaguely familiar from behind.

'I'm looking for someone who can give me some information about an incident here a week ago,' I began. The man turned. I couldn't hide my surprise. It was Steven Trentham, my old childhood friend, and Percy's son.

'Hello, Alex.'

He didn't look overjoyed to see me. In fact his eyes were full of hate. The years hadn't been kind to him. His face was harrowed, his skin dull and his once blonde hair thinning and lank.

I offered my hand. He didn't take it.

'How are you?' I rammed my hands into my

pockets, trying not to feel hurt. I wouldn't have thought Steven would have snubbed me for going to prison. Still, the Steven I had known had been a boy. It was almost thirty years ago. Much had happened since then and we had both changed.

'Fine,' he replied tersely, continuing with his work on the light aircraft.

'Didn't you go into the RAF?'

'Left in 1997.'

Silence for a moment. When it was clear the act of making conversation was going to fall to me, I said, 'You work here?' Steven had never been a great conversationalist. When we were kids I was the one who had done all the talking and the bossing around, taking advantage of my superior position as a child of the lord of the manor. If Steven wanted the last laugh he could have it now only he looked as though laughing was the last thing on his mind.

'I do pleasure flights around the Island and the odd bit of ferrying business people about.'

Do you now! I hadn't realised that Steven could fly an aeroplane. I recalled Percy's words that first day I'd seen him when I had asked how he knew that I had been released, *'Steven told me.'* How had Steven known? Perhaps he was friendly with, Angela, Miles's cleaning lady.

I said, 'Someone buzzed me in a plane a week ago last Thursday as I was walking across the airfield. I'd like to know who. Can I find out?' I had walked around so that I now faced him. I watched him carefully for a reaction. There was none.

'I doubt it.'

'Can't you check your records. He must have radioed in to say he was landing or coming over the air space or something?' I said, with exasperation and irritation.

Steven looked up. He gazed steadily at me with hazel eyes. In his right hand I could see the knuckles whiten as he tightened his grip on a wrench. There was something akin to disgust on his face.

'What is it, Steven? Don't you like associating with ex cons?' I said harshly.

He glanced away. 'It's not that.'

'What then?'

He put down the wrench and said, 'Shall we take a walk?'

I agreed with some reservations. I wasn't sure where his walk would lead; fraternising with types like Rowde had made me edgy. Was Steven about to tell me he was Andover and then try to kill me? I was glad he had relinquished the wrench.

We stepped out of the hangar and walked across the grass towards the bird sanctuary where I had taken shelter from the maniac pilot who had tried to scalp me. My heart was beating faster. Steven was silent. I couldn't believe he was Andover, and yet…

'I saw her go into your houseboat,' he said.

I froze and held my breath. I knew he must have meant Deeta.

'She didn't come out again, not until the morning,' he added.

'You were outside all night?'

'In my car.'

I groaned. On his evidence Steven could have me arrested. 'What do you want, Steven? Do you want to see me go down for murder? Wasn't embezzlement good enough? How did you do it? And why for Christ's sake?'

'That fucking war.' He spat with venom.

His answer took me by surprise. I stared at him. I could recognise a soul in torment. I recalled the carefree little boy with the sticky out ears and the wide grin. That Steven couldn't have ruined my life and my reputation. But could this one have done so? I wasn't sure.

'What happened?'

'Gulf War syndrome. I got chucked out of the RAF.'

Had the war somehow affected Steven's mind? He'd had many years to brood about it. Had it tipped him over the edge into insanity? Had all the past injustices welled up in him and focused on me?

'Why pick on me, Steven?'

'You slept with Deeta,' he rounded on me.

It wasn't the reply I had expected. I didn't see hatred in his eyes now, only a deep and inconsolable sorrow. I knew that he had been in love with Deeta.

'I stopped her at the Toll Gate café but she didn't want to speak,' he continued. 'She was angry with me for spying on her. We rowed. She stalked off along the beach and around the point. I went after her, then realised how hopeless it was. An hour later she was dead.'

'You didn't frame me?'

He stared at me confused. I had got it wrong, again. Andover wasn't Steven.

'Frame you? For what?'

'Have you told the police any of this?' I tried not to sound nervous.

'No. They haven't asked. You made love to her, didn't you?' he rounded on me. 'Did you love her?'

'No, I –'

Suddenly his fist struck my chin. I stumbled back surprised, but as I stared at him and felt the blood from my cut lip I didn't feel angry with him. I guess this was what he had asked me here for. He stepped back, and looked away. His shoulders sagged and I knew he wouldn't hit me again. I was glad. I was getting rather fed up with being everyone's punch-ball.

'That's all she was interested in, the war,' he said sorrowfully.

I scrambled up. 'Why did she want to know about the Gulf War?'

'Not that one. The Second World War,' Steven snapped.

Of course. My brain quickly reassembled the facts as Steven continued:

'She and Dad became good friends. She'd spend ages with him talking about the old days, not many people bothered. I got to know her because of it. Poor Dad. The doctor has given him some pills. I loved her, not like some people who used her and thought nothing of it.'

'I'm sorry.'

He turned away and began walking back to the hangar. 'I'll see what I can find out about that plane buzzing you,' he called over his shoulder.

I hurried back to the houseboat, taking the footpath behind the village at the back of my mother's house and coming out by the Pilot Boat Inn. Even then I couldn't avoid the small huddled groups of villagers and dog walkers. I caught snatches of conversation about Deeta's death. Someone said that the police had set up an incident room in the village hall. I was worried that if the police questioned Steven he'd tell them about Deeta and me. I couldn't afford to lose any time sitting in a police interview room. Where the hell was Rowde? Why didn't he get in touch? Perhaps he'd be waiting for me back at the houseboat. He wasn't, Scarlett was.

'Where have you been?' she declared. 'I've got some news for you about that blonde woman. You'll have to come with me though. I can't leave Mum alone.'

Ruby was staring at the television, her hands clasping her straw handbag.

Scarlett glanced at her mother and then at me. She spoke in hushed tones. 'I was cleaning Deeta's room in the hotel the day before she was killed. I had to take Mum with me. I can't leave her here, can I?'

She glared at me as if I was going to chastise her. I wondered where all this was leading.

'Usually Mum's pretty good. She just sits there muttering to herself or singing. I was called away to another room; a guest wanted his breakfast brought up and there was no one else to do it so I had to leave Mum, only for a few minutes. I didn't realise she'd taken it until yesterday, *after* I heard that Deeta had been killed.'

'Taken what?'

'This.' And she stretched across me to the bread bin which she flipped open. She pulled out a photograph in a silver frame. As she straightened up she looked at me and I felt something jump between us that startled her as much as it did me. She frowned and thrust the photograph into my hands.

I gazed down at it. I wasn't sure what I expected but it wasn't the photograph of a young man in his early twenties, handsome with a square jaw and broad smile, tall and slender. He was dressed in a lounge suit, shirt and tie. In the background was a chalk cliff and sea. It looked remarkably like Whitecliff Bay to me. Judging by the type of photograph and the clothes I would have said it had been taken in the 1930s.

'Who is it?' And what, more to the point, was this to do with me?

Scarlett rolled her eyes. 'How the devil should I know? Mum thinks it's someone called Max. I've only just managed to get it away from her. They'll think I've stolen it. I can't tell the police, you know how their minds work. I'll lose my job. I don't know what to do.' She thrust a hand through her hair, which was now copper with black streaks.

I was flattered that she had confided in me. Her trust warmed my aching heart.

'Let's see who it is.'

I prised open the back and extracted the photograph whilst Scarlett kept an eye on her mother.

'It *is* Max.'

Scarlett looked shocked. I didn't blame her. We'd both dismissed everything Ruby said as nonsense. If Ruby was right about this could she possibly be right about someone pushing my mother down the stairs?

I read aloud the writing on the back of the photograph. 'Maximilian Weber, Whitecliff Bay 1938.'

'Weber, that was Deeta's surname,' Scarlett said. 'This must be her grandfather. She was too young for it to be her father, and, besides, he's arrived at the hotel. I saw him check in last night. Did you know she was German?'

It explained her accent and maybe her conversations with Percy. 'She said something about her grandfather being here at the beginning of the war. Perhaps that's when Ruby knew him. Steven Trentham told me Deeta used to talk about the war endlessly with Percy.'

Scarlett scowled. 'You've spoken to Steven?'

'Yes.' I could see she looked uncomfortable and wondered why.

She turned round and began to fill the kettle. 'Steven followed her from your houseboat. I saw him.'

'He's just told me.'

'Did he also tell you that we were once married?' She spun round. 'I can see not, judging by your shocked expression and your gaping mouth. I suppose it surprises you that someone wanted to marry me.'

'I never said –'

'You don't have to.'

'Why are you always so defensive?' I cried, exasperated.

'Takes years to perfect and with a father like mine I got plenty of chance to practise.'

Her tone was light but I could hear the pain behind the words. I saw a life of pretending she didn't care what they said about her father. Her hostility was a shield to prevent her from being hurt. I wondered if her eccentric hair colour and style of dress were also used as a kind of barrier to stop people from getting too close.

'Do you think Steven killed her?' I asked.

'I don't know.' And that, I could see, was eating her up. 'He was always so jealous, so possessive. It suffocated me. He was even worse after the Gulf War. It wasn't his fault. He started to drink.'

'Scarlett, Scarlett,' came a plaintive wailing.

'Where are you? Why has everyone left me? Where's Teddy.'

Scarlett brushed against me as she went to Ruby. I felt something stir inside me that was more than sexual attraction.

'The bombs they frighten me. Do they frighten you?' Ruby said.

'Sometimes.' Scarlett turned to me. 'These days she lives so much in the past that she hardly knows who I am. Sometimes she asks me when her real daughter is coming back.'

'Can't you get help?'

'You mean put her in a home,' she rounded on me again, her eyes blazing.

'No, I didn't mean that,' I said wearily. 'Look, I think it's best if you say nothing about the photograph. They might not even know that it's missing.'

Scarlett said, 'There's something else I think you should know. Deeta was on your houseboat before you came back.'

'I know. She found the door open and discovered the place had been ransacked.'

'I mean she was inside for a long time before you showed up.'

'How long?' I asked, suddenly suspicious.

'About half an hour, forty minutes.'

'Are you sure?' I was struck by the thought that

maybe she had ransacked the place. But why would she do that? What could she have been looking for? Had someone told her I could possibly have three million pounds? Was that why she had been so willing? Had she been after my money, rather than my body? Deeta had made a play for me from the start. Deeta had been in Brading church when the aeroplane had buzzed me. Did she have any connection with what had happened to me?

Scarlett said, 'I thought you might also like to know that her hotel room was trashed.'

Was it indeed! Had her killer thought she'd discovered something on my houseboat and had taken it back to her hotel? What though? Did this have anything to do with Andover? Was I wasting time thinking this? It didn't feel like it. If Gus wasn't the link between Andover's three victims then who and what was? Deeta was a link between me and Steven Trentham, and Steven with my past. Steven could fly an aeroplane and Scarlett said he was possessive and possibly even unbalanced. I had seen that and could still feel his punch on my chin. I had ruled Steven out, but could I? I thought it was about time I had a word with Percy.

# CHAPTER 13

I found Percy on the beach. His forlorn little figure was staring out to sea. We were alone except for a woman walking her West Highland terrier the other side of the long thin pier that stretched out to sea, on the end of which was the lifeboat station.

'Do you want a tea or coffee?' I asked, jerking my head in the direction of the café to my right.

'No thanks. Let's sit up the top there.'

We climbed the slope up to the small car park by the toilets and Royal National Lifeboat Institution shop. On the bank of grass to the left of it were a handful of seats. We took the second one of the benches facing seaward. Percy had lost some of his sparkle and his breathing was a little laboured. He looked off-colour, a dejected figure now rather than a comical one. I suddenly realised he was an old man.

It was mid morning and low tide. The sea washed gently onto the sand, and across the Solent in a distance haze I could just make out the shores of Hayling Island. It looked like summer but there was a fresh wind that reminded me it was still only April. A small fishing boat was chugging steadily towards Sandown Bay. I thought of Westnam and the person who might discover his sea-worn body. The crabs and sea life would have made a meal of him and it wouldn't be a pretty sight.

'It's a sad world,' the old man said quietly and wearily, echoing my thoughts. 'And the more I see of it the sadder it gets. She was such a lovely girl.'

'It must have been terrible for you to find her.'

'It was, though I've seen worse in the war.' He glanced at me. 'I've seen things that would make your stomach heave and your legs turn to jelly and I weren't nothing but a boy then. Seeing her lying in a heap on the beach brought it all back to me. I thought I'd forgotten it, but I hadn't. I suppose you just push it away and get on with life, well leastways that was what we used to do in them days. Now it's all counselling. Don't do no good if you ask me. It hasn't helped our Steven much. Poor Scarlett had a terrible time of it; no wonder she couldn't stick it. I don't blame her for wanting shot of him. But he seems to be getting himself together now. He's been back with me for ten years and buying that plane a few years ago has given him something else to think about. Doesn't do to brood on things.'

'He told me that he and Deeta were very close.'

The old man eyed me sadly. 'Wishful thinking on Steven's part. She were no more interested in him than she were in me. Oh, I liked to fool meself just like our Steven did, I mean a pretty girl like her hanging on your every word, looking at you with those big blue eyes, bound to go to your heart and loins. Though the loins bit is beyond me now, more's the pity.' He smiled and I saw something of the old Percy bouncing back. I was glad.

'She was writing a book about the war, I believe.'

Percy nodded. 'Yes. She wanted to know what part I played in it. Told her I was a boy runner. She was very interested in the radar station at Ventnor. Did you know it was the only radar station to be destroyed in the war?'

I did. I'd heard the story so many times I could recite it backwards. I needed to get Percy talking about Steven but I could see there would be no hurrying him.

Percy continued, 'I saw the pylons go up in 1938, you know. It must have been about the same time your granddad built that folly of his.'

I remembered seeing a diary for 1938 amongst my mother's possessions. Is that what Deeta wanted *if* she had been the person to have searched my houseboat. But what significance could it have? I recalled her gentle questioning of me in between our lovemaking. She had asked me about my mother's childhood during the war and I had thought nothing of it. In fact, I couldn't tell her much, my mother had rarely spoken of it. Was that diary from 1938 still on the houseboat? Though what connection it might have had with Andover, or Steven come to that, I couldn't even guess.

Percy continued, 'Your granddad knew a war was coming. Most of us thought he was a bit eccentric. Chamberlain said there was peace. But Edward Hardley was right in the end. Of course we didn't know the reason for the pylons then, it was all hush hush. By 1939 there were these great big tall steel masts and wooden towers on the Downs. The radar station was bombed in

1940, along with Portsmouth Dockyard. The Spitfires went up. You should have seen them.' Percy's eyes were shining at the excitement of the memory. 'They shot the hell out of them Germans, but the bombs still got through. I was running for the firemen, taking buckets of water up there, but it were like pissing on an inferno. Bloody useless.'

His eyes swivelled to his right. He couldn't see St Boniface Down above Ventnor from here, not physically but in his mind I knew he could. Time to bring him back on track.

'About Steven, has he –'

'It was completely destroyed, you know. We were lucky though. Only one soldier got hurt. Deeta was really interested in the radar station and curious about your grandfather. She wanted to look inside the folly. She asked Steven about that many a time. She was disappointed you'd sold the house. I often wondered why she was so interested.'

Now, come to think of it, I was curious too. Suddenly I had the strange sensation that someone was watching us. I glanced behind; there was only a woman in one of the bungalows pottering about in her front garden. I felt uneasy.

'Perhaps it was because her grandfather was here at the start of the war. Now about –'

'Was he? She never said,' Percy said surprised.

'Maybe she didn't like to. Not to you, Percy. She was German and her –'

'She were German?' Percy cried.

His rheumy eyes were wide and I felt sure he had lost even more of his colour. His hands began to tremble in his lap.

'You didn't know?'

He shook his head vigorously. 'She never said she was a Jerry.'

'It's all right, Percy, you didn't tell her any secrets,' I said, smiling, 'The war was a long time ago.'

'Not to me it isn't. It's yesterday. And it was to your mum too and poor old Ruby.'

He looked as if he was about to cry. Hastily, I said, 'I'm sorry, I didn't think. Of course there must be painful memories for you. It's just that Deeta is… was young.' I was about to add that she was also a historian, only I was beginning to doubt whether that were true. I said, 'The war is history to a lot of people.'

'More's the pity,' he replied sharply. 'As you get older, young man, you tend to live in the past because there's more of it than the future. Are you sure she was German?'

'Yes. I think her grandfather must have been too: Maximilian…'

I didn't think Percy could go any paler but at the mention of that name his skin was almost transparent. Now I was very curious.

'What is it, Percy?'

He removed his grubby white baseball cap and ran a hand over his silver hair. His eyes shifted from right to left. It would have been comical if it weren't for the fact that I could see he was genuinely upset.

'I'd never have told her if I'd known she was German.' His voice was barely above a whisper. 'She was so good at listening. Bugger her.'

He startled me. I didn't think I had ever heard him swear before. He fiddled with his cap in his lap.

'Don't upset yourself, Percy. You didn't do anything wrong.' I tried to reassure him, but he wasn't having it.

I reeled back at the intensity of the look he turned on me. Only then did it click that there was more going on here than I had realised. Despite all my problems I found myself interested, and deep down somewhere inside me a sixth sense was telling me that there was something I should know about. Why and what I could do with the information I had no idea.

'Percy,' I began slowly and steadily. 'Did you *know* Maximilian Weber?'

'Weber?'

A loud explosion filled the air and sent the Canada geese and seagulls squawking. Percy clutched his chest and almost jumped out of his seat whilst I didn't do much better. I put my hand on his arm, 'It's only the call for the lifeboat.'

Percy knew this but I hoped my touch was reassuring. He took a deep breath and swivelled to look at me.

'Who was he, Percy?' I asked quietly. 'Ruby knew him.'

'Reckon we should walk for a bit.'

'OK.' I rose, curbing my impatience. Before we had gone far I could hear cars screeching into the car park and turned to see men race down to the lifeboat station.

We stood for a moment watching the lifeboat launch, its orange bow thrusting through the blue green sea heading towards the Cardinal Buoy and a container ship, above which hovered a helicopter. Slowly we began walking towards Whitecliff Bay. I knew I wouldn't be able to hurry Percy. I guessed this tale had been a long time coming.

'There were three of them, only he weren't called Weber then. Maximilian Webb was his name, but I guess it was the same man.'

I could see from Percy's manner that he *knew* it was.

Percy continued, 'Max, Hugo and your grandfather, Edward.'

Ruby had been right. Nevertheless I wondered why she had mistaken me for Hugo instead of my grandfather.

'I looked up to them. Thought the sun shone out of their backsides,' Percy added. 'I was only a boy, just a bit older than your mother, Olivia, or Livvy as me and Ruby called her. She and Ruby were about thirteen when the war broke out. I was fifteen. We used to lark around on the beach in the summer or in your grandfather's gardens at Bembridge House. It was a lovely place and me and Ruby thought we were in heaven being special friends of them up at the big house, like. But Livvy was never stuck up and neither was your grandmother.' He paused and gazed around fearful.

'What is it, Percy?'

'One evening I was behind those rocks over there and the three men were walking along the beach. I weren't following them or anything, just larking about.' He hesitated. I could see that wasn't the truth. He continued. 'They came round the bend and I ducked out of sight. They stopped about where we are now.'

And we did the same. I gazed out to sea. The lifeboat had almost reached the container ship.

'I heard Edward say. "It's got to stop." Then Hugo said, "We've only just started. The situation is getting worse in Germany by the day. There are hundreds of them wanting to get out. We've got it all set up." Your grandfather said, "I don't think it's right, taking their money like that." Hugo laughed. "We're doing them a favour, and the Nazis a public service. The Nazis want the Jews out and the Jews will pay anything to get out. You just bring the boat across to France. Max and I will do the rest." Percy paused and took a breath.

'What year was this?'

'It was winter. Must have been either late 1938, or early part of 1939.'

I thought of that diary again. 'My mother was with you, wasn't she? Here on the beach. She overheard them?'

He looked sheepish and nodded. 'We weren't up to nothing, just talking.'

I believed him; times had changed.

'We didn't understand what they were talking about. We were just kids. It wasn't until after the war it all came out what Hitler did to the Jews.'

But my mother had written it in her diary. Was that all she had written? Was it still on the houseboat, or had Deeta found it? Was that why she was killed? Was that why she had searched my houseboat? I couldn't see how it mattered? There was nothing wrong with what the three men had been doing, unless of course they had been helping the Jews to emigrate illegally for a fee, which seemed likely. Even then history had shown they had been saving them from a terrible fate. I said as much to Percy.

He turned to stare at me. I could see there was more.

'After the war had started, and the radar station had been attacked in 1940, I was back here on the beach, walking home. It was dusk. There'd been an attack on the mainland and you could see the sky alight with fire. I remember thinking poor buggers. I stumbled on Edward and Max. They were arguing. I don't know what about. I heard Max say, "I'm going to the authorities." Your grandfather strode off and that was the last anyone saw of him. He disappeared along with his boat. Drowned, though they never found his body.'

That had been a constant concern of my grandmother's. What Percy was telling me had all happened a long time ago, but the past, as Percy had reminded me, is never very far away.

'What happened to Max?'

'No idea. Never saw nor heard of him again. But if you now say he was German…'

'I don't know if he was for sure, but Deeta was and Weber is a German name. Perhaps Max was English, went to Germany after the war, married and settled down there.'

'Could have done,' Percy mumbled. I could see he wasn't convinced, and neither was I.

We turned round and started walking back. The lifeboat had reached the container ship, but we couldn't see what was happening. It was too far away.

'He didn't sound German,' Percy went on. 'They all talked nice, you know, posh like.'

Percy fell silent. His wrinkled face was glum. His eyes troubled. I thought over what he had told me. Had they really been helping to rescue Jews from Hitler's clutches, not only in 1939, but later, after Hitler had closed the borders? Percy was talking about overhearing this second conversation after the radar station was bombed, which was after Dunkirk. Northern France would have been occupied. It would have been highly dangerous. What did Max mean about going to the authorities? As I had said to Percy, it was a long time ago. I brought my mind back to the present. What I had to ask Percy was delicate, and I didn't want to cause the old man any further distress, but I had to know.

'Percy, did you see how Deeta was killed?' I asked gently.

Percy shuddered. 'Strangled with bare hands by the looks of it.'

Like Westnam. So someone had been facing her. Had it been someone she knew? Or had it been a stranger who had struck up a casual acquaintance with her and then attacked her?

'Was her rucksack beside her?' She'd been carrying it when she had left my houseboat.

Percy frowned in thought. 'Yes. It was open and some of her things had spilled out onto the beach.'

'Did you see a small maroon book, like a diary?' I didn't hold out much hope of him remembering in the shock of discovering Deeta's body.

'Can't say that I did.'

I would need to return to the houseboat and check if it was still there. We had reached the car park. I was worried about Percy. He was very pale and shaky.

'Would you like me to see you home?' I volunteered, but he refused my offer.

'I'll be all right,' he replied sadly and began to shuffle away. He had only gone a few paces when I hailed him.

'You mentioned the three men: Max, Edward and Hugo. My grandfather was drowned. Max disappeared. What happened to Hugo?'

Percy turned to face me; his lined old face was drawn and fearful. 'Hugo Wildern was hanged, for being a German spy.'

## CHAPTER 14

Percy's words gnawed away at me. It would have made more sense if Max had been arrested for treason, not Hugo though I was viewing this with the benefit of hindsight. Max, I guessed from Percy's conversation, had betrayed Hugo to the authorities, but for what? Telling the Germans about the radar station? It was possible. Had Max been the spy and not Hugo, which seemed more likely. In that case Hugo had been falsely betrayed. But what did this have to do with me? Nothing I told myself but still I headed for the library.

Before I reached it I glanced across the road at the village hall. The doors were open and a policeman and policewoman stood at the entrance talking to a couple of middle-aged men. Opposite, outside the bakery, a small crowd had gathered, they were gossiping and glancing across at the police officers. The little coffee shop in the bakery was doing a roaring trade, as was Bembridge itself. Far from putting people off coming to the village the murder had attracted more visitors.

I could find no record of Hugo on the Internet for having been tried and hanged for treason. Four people had been convicted under the High Treason Act: William Joyce, commonly known as Lord Haw Haw, John Amery, Walter Purdy and Thomas Cooper. Theodore Schurch was convicted under the Treachery Act of 1940. Of these men Purdy and Cooper had their sentence commuted and were eventually released. Amery was executed on 19 December 1945, Joyce on 3 January 1946, both at Wandsworth Prison, and Schurch on 4 January 1946 at Pentonville Prison.

I could check with the Public Record Office but Percy must have got it wrong. It was probably the gossip at the time. Percy always did like to embellish. I looked under German spies and agents but whatever happened to Hugo Wildern it was never recorded.

I glanced at my watch and saw that it was time I made for Camp Hill Prison. The thought brought me out in a cold sweat. Long before I reached the prison gates my heart was pounding violently. I stepped inside the magnolia-painted visitors' room and my stomach heaved at the prison smell and the fact that I was once again incarcerated. I told myself that at least I could walk out of here a free man. Yet, I wasn't free. Rowde was pulling the strings and I could do nothing but jerk in his direction.

Ray greeted me with smile and a 'what the hell are you doing here?' kind of look whilst the screws eyed me with suspicion. When I had telephoned to arrange the visit I had made up a story about Ray asking me to call on his brother in Portsmouth who had Multiple Sclerosis (that much was true, apart from my visiting him) and that Ray's brother had pleaded with me to pass on a personal message for forgiveness. They'd argued bitterly and fought physically before Ray had been caught and sentenced for burglary, and it was time to kiss and make up. I was sure they didn't believe a word of it but here I was, so I didn't care much what they believed.

'Who worked you over?' were Ray's first words.

'Rowde, or rather one of his thugs.'

Ray raised his eyebrows. The screws hadn't commented on my battered appearance.

'Rowde's after me for the money I don't have,' I said, making sure the prison officer was far enough away not to hear my lowered tones. 'I was banged up with him in Brixton for a while. It wasn't a very pleasant experience.'

'He's a head case. A vicious sod.'

'With a long memory, it seems. He wants the money and unless I give it to him by Tuesday morning he's threatening to harm my sons. I believe him. I've got to find out where that money is. It's my only chance, short of killing Rowde, and I'll do that if I have to and willingly serve time for it if it means my boys are safe.'

Ray rubbed his large fleshy nose. His malleable face screwed up with thought or concern, or both, I wasn't quite sure. Thief he might be but he wasn't, and never had been, violent. I told him about DCI Clipton's heart attack and Joe's murder but I said nothing about Westnam. Then I told him that I'd been to see Roger Brookes' widow and daughter.

'The daughter, Joanne, is living with a man called Jamie Redman. I asked about him in the local pub and learnt that he's a "flash git" according to the barmaid, and not that well liked. He moved to the Cotswolds with Joanne three years ago and doesn't quite blend in with the local gentry and county set.'

'So?' Ray took a cigarette from one of the packets I had brought him and lit up.

'He smells dirty. The barmaid says he's into importing and exporting classic cars. Joanne's well off in her own right. Daddy sold his business to a conglomerate and she split the money with her mother. She's not right either, Ray. The whole set-up stinks. Mother and daughter have a secret that they're very afraid I might discover.'

Ray squinted his eyes as he exhaled. 'And how will this lead you to the money?'

'Christ knows!' I cried, flinging myself back in the chair and pushing a hand through my hair. The screw eyed me with suspicion. Ease up I told myself. I tried to relax and look natural. 'If I could find out why Andover could so easily blackmail Brookes it might lead me to him. I need you to ask around about Jamie Redman. Is he clean? Has he any dodgy associates? Is he known to anyone?' Ray may be inside but there was a hell of a lot he could find out by asking certain inmates.

'You've got it.'

'And quickly, Ray. I don't have much time.'

'I'll call you as soon as I can.'

'Good, your brother will be pleased.'

'Yeah, thought he might be. Is our time up already, Mr Harris? Doesn't it fly when you're enjoying yourself.' Ray scraped back his chair. 'Thanks for the fags, Alex, and the message. You'd better give me your number so that I can call you and find out how Eric's doing. He's going into hospital, Mr Harris.'

'Oh yeah?' Harris didn't look convinced. That was his problem. As long as Ray could get to a phone then I didn't care what he thought.

I gave him Scarlett's mobile number, told Ray that he'd get my neighbour and that she would come and get me or take a message. I could see that he read between the lines, incorrectly as it happened. All I had to do now was tell Scarlett.

First, though, I dived into Newport and bought myself a mobile phone. I had resisted for as long as I could, but I was getting weary of finding a pay phone and felt the urgent need to keep in touch with Scarlett. If Ray had any news to impart, I needed access to it immediately.

I drove back to the houseboat checking my mirror continually for any signs that I was being followed. I wasn't. The police didn't seem interested in me, but still I rounded the bend onto the Embankment cautiously and scanned the horizon for any sign of police cars. There were none and only one car I didn't recognise parked in the lay by opposite my houseboat. It was an expensive BMW with tinted windows. It didn't look much like a police detective's car and it wasn't Detective Chief Inspector Crowder's.

As soon as I stepped into my small forecourt I could see that the front door had once again been forced open. It hadn't taken much because after the break in I had only put a couple of bolts on the inside. I was beginning to wonder why I bothered. I might as well leave it open.

My heart started knocking against my ribs. Was I about to be arrested? Maybe I should simply turn and drive away. But what if Rowde was inside waiting for me? I couldn't risk not seeing him. I had to know that my family were still safe.

I pushed open the door. Rowde was picking over the debris of the lounge that I hadn't bothered to tidy up. Fury seized me at the sight of his smug countenance and I lunged forward shouting:

'Where are they, you bastard?'

Marble man struck me before I had even reached spitting distance of Rowde. I fell heavily to the ground, jarring my back on something. Winded though I was I still managed to gasp, 'If you so much as hurt one hair of their head I'll –'

'What? Beat me to a pulp? I doubt that.' Rowde laughed.

Marble man looked like he was coming back for seconds; I tensed myself but Rowde shouted, 'Leave him. I think he's got the message.'

'I've got two more days, not counting today, to get your money. Why have you taken Vanessa and the boys now?' I struggled up, trying not to wince at the pain.

'The deadline's been cancelled.'

'What?' My head came up and my stomach heaved. The houseboat swam before me. My heart was pounding rapidly and I could hardly catch my breath. I looked up at Rowde's smug expression. My eyes swivelled to marble man; fists clenched, he looked as if he was eagerly anticipating beating the hell out of me. Now I was praying that the police had found out about Deeta being on my houseboat and that they'd walk through that door. But the cavalry had never come to my rescue before, so why should it now?

'I'll get the money for you. Just let them go,' I urged.

Rowde ambled around the dishevelled room finally settling himself opposite me on the bench seat.

'I need time,' I pressed.

'Time is one thing you don't have, Alex, and neither do I. I want the money now.'

I had to tell him about the plan I had hatched

with Gus on our return from Guernsey, but I had to convince him it was the truth. I hesitated, looked distressed, (which was easy, because I was) and finally, after seeming to wrestle with my conscience, said, 'It's in a Swiss numbered account. I have to travel to Zurich to get it.' I held Rowde's gaze. He looked sceptical. 'I could give permission for it to be transferred to you, but that way the money could be traced by the police. Still if that's what you want, it makes no difference to me…'

'We'll go to Zurich.'

'Only one problem, Rowde, I can't travel on my passport. I'm out on licence. They'll stop me. And I'm being followed by the police.'

My heart gave a little whoop of joy as marble man looked decidedly uncomfortable.

Rowde glared at me. 'How do you know?'

I laughed scornfully. Why hadn't I thought of this before? *To fight scum you've got to act like scum* – Ray's words.

'Give me credit for learning something whilst I was in prison, Rowde. I wasn't always banged up with you.' I wondered if he'd get the insult but he didn't. 'I not only know how to smell and spot a copper a hundred yards away, but I also know how to invest money. I'll get you your three million plus interest and then you can bugger off into the sunset and leave my boys alone. I might even join you. No, on second thoughts you're far too crude for me. Demanding money with menace is not my style. I don't need it when I can use a computer.'

I saw him thinking over my words and the light dawned in his eyes. I don't think I'd have been surprised to see pound signs roll in his pupils like a gaming machine.

I said, 'I'll need a false passport to get out of the country. I take it you can organise that for me?' I sat back and crossed my legs. I almost wished I smoked. I was doing my best Humphrey Bogart impersonation. 'And I don't want ugly guts there tagging along. It's just you and me, Rowde.'

Marble man stepped forward, but a look from Rowde and he froze.

I had Rowde convinced. 'There's another condition. I hand the money over *after* you let Vanessa and my sons go, and I have spoken to them on the telephone, and Gus has confirmed they're all right. If they're not, or you foul up in any way, then the three million will stay exactly where it is. What do you want the most Rowde, money or murder?' I held my breath.

After a moment Rowde nodded. 'OK, when?'

'How quickly can you get the passport?'

He thought a moment. 'Monday morning.'

'OK, call me as soon as you've got a name for me and then I'll arrange the flights. You can meet me at the airport with the passports. I'll telephone the bank to let them know I'm coming, and if you think that you can beat the account number out of me, and then just show up and forge my signature, think again. They also need my fingerprints and I don't think even you'd get away with carrying in my dead fingers.'

I was bullshitting like mad but it fooled Rowde. I wasn't sure what I'd do when we got to Zurich and I didn't much care, as long as Vanessa and the boys were unharmed.

'Now I want to speak to them. Get them on the phone.'

'That's not part of the deal.'

'There's no money then and the police will be here in a minute.'

Rowde was punching in a number before I'd finished speaking. He spoke a few words and then handed over his mobile.

'Vanessa!' My heart leapt into my throat. The blood was pounding in my ears.

'What's happening, Alex?'

'I can't tell you now, but soon it will be over. Are you OK?'

'Yes, but Alex –'

Rowde snatched the phone away. I said, 'I'm warning you Rowde if you hurt them –'

'I will if you don't show up at the airport. Now give me your mobile number.'

I jotted it down for him.

Rowde hesitated at the door. 'Barry, see if the filth are out there.'

'I doubt you'll spot them,' I said.

'Like you, Barry and I also have a good nose for coppers. Anyway they can't get anything on me, this is just a social visit catching up on old times. All that crap about being framed, why didn't you just say in the first place? It would have saved you a beating.'

'I didn't want to spoil Barry's fun.' Rowde had reached the gate when I said, 'Did you kill the girl?'

He turned back, surprised. 'What girl?'

'The blonde one.'

'Don't know any blondes.'

I didn't believe him.

I turned my attention to the chaos in my bedroom, in particular my mother's belongings. I wasn't surprised to find that her diary for 1938 had gone, but I was surprised to discover that the photograph of me with my telescope had. I searched in vain and could only draw the conclusion that Deeta must have taken it. Why should she want a photograph of me? There was only one reason and that was prompted by something Percy had said. My mother and I had been standing in front of the folly. I couldn't think why Deeta should be interested in that; it was just bricks and cement, a great empty chasm of a place that had been stuffed full of junk when I had been a boy. And, as the police hadn't yet come to question me, whoever had killed Deeta must have taken both items from her.

I knocked on Scarlett's door.

'Do you know if the Asletts are at home this weekend?' I asked stepping inside. I had remembered that Scarlett was their cleaner.

'Why? Are you thinking of calling on them?' she said with a hint of sarcasm.

'Not them. Bembridge House.'

She frowned puzzled. I guess I owed her an explanation and by her expression she wasn't going to give me the information I wanted until I gave her one.

'I need to get inside the folly. I suspect there is a key to it inside the house.'

'Why on earth do you want to get in there?'

'It's better if you don't know.'

'Oh, big boy stuff, is it?' she flashed.

'No. I just don't want you going the same way as Deeta.'

After a moment she said. 'OK. I understand your reasoning and appreciate your concern, but if it's anything to do with this Max then I want to know about it. Besides I think you owe me a couple of favours.'

She put her hands on her ample hips and glared at me. I had to smile to myself. She wasn't going to give me the information I needed without a fight, and she was right. I did owe her.

I told her what Percy had said about Hugo, Max and Edward, and about the missing diary and photograph.

'I need to see if there is a reason why Deeta was so interested in my grandfather's folly, and why the photograph of my mother and me taken outside it has gone missing.'

'What on earth can any of this have to do with whoever framed you?'

'It probably doesn't, but for want of anywhere else to look I might as well give it a go.' I didn't tell her about Rowde kidnapping my family, and my looming deadline.

She assessed me for a moment. Then said, 'Let's go take a look then.'

'Not you,' I cried alarmed.

'You bet me. You can't get into the house without me.' She dangled a bunch of keys at me. 'Unless you want to knock me out and steal them from me, then I'll call the police.'

'OK,' I agreed reluctantly, but knowing that she wouldn't.

'The Asletts are away for the weekend. I can't leave Mum alone here so we'll drop her at Percy's on our way. Come on, Mum.'

Before I could protest Scarlett had Ruby's coat on and was locking the door behind us. 'We'll go in my car. Mum's used to it.'

Stifling my impatience and annoyance I let Scarlett have her way. A few minutes later she was unlocking Bembridge House. I hadn't had time to consider how I would feel stepping back inside my childhood home and now that I did I was overwhelmed with such a great sadness that I couldn't move and my breath came in a tight shudder. Perhaps it was the sight of the staircase and the picture in my mind of my poor mother tumbling down it to her death; perhaps it was the thought that this would have been my family home if it hadn't been for Andover; perhaps it was both but for a moment I felt like crawling away to a corner and howling. The moment passed and I sought refuge where I had done so many times in the last few years: in my anger.

'The key to the folly is in the kitchen,' Scarlett said, swiftly crossing the hall.

I followed her into a room that was so completely different to my mother's that I might have been in another house. I was certainly in a different time zone. It looked as though it had been transplanted from NASA, all chrome and angles. I was glad. I didn't want to be reminded of my mother moving around the warm, comfortable room of my childhood, with its oak dressers and aga.

I followed Scarlett out into the gardens. It was late afternoon and it had started raining but neither of us took much notice of the weather.

'Give me the key,' I demanded. Scarlett thrust it in my hand.

It was a big heavy old-fashioned type, which I inserted and turned not knowing what to expect. The lock was well oiled and the heavy oak door swung open fairly easily.

'There's a light, here.' I reached to my right and suddenly the place was lit by a single overhead electric light bulb that cast eerie shadows around the edges of the domed-shaped building.

I shivered. Not just from the chill interior but at the boyhood memories. Once I had been locked in here by mistake. Steven had done it whilst we had been playing. Now all those sensations returned: my clammy skin, the panicky breathing, the oppressiveness, and the impression that I was being watched.

Scarlett broke the spell. 'It's just a junk store.'

'What did you expect? Treasure?'

'Would have been nice.'

The Asletts were using it to store their garden furniture. There were sun loungers, a garden table and parasol, a barbecue, some very old planks of wood that I was sure had been in the far corner when I had been a boy, and what looked like a wooden mast from a sailing boat with some furled up sails.

Scarlett said, 'What are you looking for?'

'My grandfather built this as an air raid shelter, which means there must be a room underneath here. Somewhere his family could hide if the bombs came.'

'Great! We've got to lug this stuff around now.'

'You don't have to stay.'

'You're not getting rid of me that easily.' And she set too with vigour, ignoring the dirt and the insects. I couldn't see Vanessa or Deeta doing that. I found to my surprise that I was rather glad she was with me. It was good not to be alone.

Finally we found it, a trapdoor in the far corner covered with dirt, dust and the old wooden planks. I was surprised I had never found it as a boy, but I suppose being shut in here once was enough to make me singularly uncurious for the rest of my life – until now.

With a pounding heart I said, 'Give me a hand.'

We grunted and groaned as we pulled at the handle. It was very stiff but slowly it began to give way. The Asletts had never found this and certainly Deeta, and whoever was working with her hadn't either. I could smell the earth, dust and decay. There was a black hole beneath us.

'I should have brought a torch.'

'There's one in the house. I'll fetch it.'

Lying down flat on my stomach, I stared down at the blackness. Reaching out with my hands I could feel a ladder. God alone knew if the rungs were safe. I'd have to chance it. I didn't believe in buried treasure but I did wonder if this might be where the three men had stashed their money from helping the Jews to escape Hitler's clutches, hence Deeta's interest.

Scarlett was back by the time it occurred to me that whoever had killed Deeta and taken the photograph and diary, could be here at any moment to kill us.

I shone the powerful beam inside the cavity. Yes, there was a ladder. The rungs might be rotten but it wasn't far to the bottom so if I fell I doubted I'd do much damage to myself. Tentatively I climbed down backwards as I would have done on a boat, feeling for each rung carefully, testing it before putting my weight on it. At last I dropped to the floor. I was in a small room about ten feet square. I wouldn't have liked to cower in here whilst the bombs fell! I'd rather have taken my chances up top.

It was clear that nobody had been down here for years. I shuddered as I heard the scurrying of rats. My flesh crawled and it was all I could do to force myself to stay put.

'Have you found anything?' Scarlett called out to me.

'Just a load of old dirt and rats.'

I didn't want her coming down and knowing Scarlett she would. I hoped the rats would put her off.

My beam searched the depths of the room. There was a bigger heap of dirt in the far right hand corner. I stepped towards it, feeling my heart knocking against my ribs. I felt very cold. I took a couple of deep breaths. I could hear the wind rising outside. It wasn't dirt. It looked like shards of cloth. With my torch I slowly peeled it back knowing what I would see before I saw it. I was right. I climbed back up to Scarlett.

'Well?'

'Bones. Human,' I said, brushing myself down.

'My God! Whose?'

I looked steadily at her face smeared with dirt, her brown eyes wide with surprise. I didn't know whose but I could take a guess. 'Either my grandfather's or Hugo's.'

# CHAPTER 15

'You can't leave him there. DNA will tell you who he is,' she said.

'I know that, but I've got no choice. Not yet, at least.'

We were making our way back to Percy's house. 'What do you mean?'

'I have to find Andover first. I suggest you try and forget about it, Scarlett. Just for a while. I'll tell the police when I'm ready.'

After a moment she shrugged and said, 'OK, it's your business.'

It took a while for Percy to answer the door and when he did clearly all was not well with him. Scarlett quickly waved me in. Percy looked near to collapse. He staggered back into a small old-fashioned living room where Ruby was gazing rather blankly at the television set. Ashen faced and trembling he sank into an armchair. He looked at least ten years older than when I had seen him this morning.

'What is it?' I asked anxiously, crossing to him.

'It's Steven. He's been arrested for murder.'

Scarlett glared at me as if it was my fault. I knew what she was thinking. If Deeta hadn't been on my houseboat, if I hadn't made love to her, then Steven wouldn't have followed her and be suspected of murder. Steven would tell them about Deeta and me, obviously. How long did I have before the police came for me?

'When, Percy?' I asked.

'About half an hour ago. I didn't know what to do. They said someone had seen him and Deeta arguing outside the café. Steven couldn't have killed her, could he?' He appealed to Scarlett.

The pleading in his eyes tore at my heart. Doubt was eating him up.

Scarlett took his hand. 'Of course not, Percy. They'll soon realise they've got it wrong.'

'They didn't with Alex.'

Scarlett dashed me a look full of fear. Percy's words, and the despair in his watery old eyes filled me with dread. Steven had a very powerful motive for killing Deeta: jealousy. Scarlett would testify she had seen me drive away. Percy was right to be afraid.

'Has Steven got a solicitor?' I asked.

'You mean Mr Kerry in the High Street.'

'No. We need one who specialises in criminal law. I'll call Miles.'

I stepped into the narrow hall. When Miles answered I quickly explained what had happened, leaving out the bit about Rowde holding my family hostage and the skeleton in the folly.

'Could you come over now?' I glanced at my watch. It was nearly 6.30pm. He could catch the seven o' clock sailing.

'Of course. What about you? If the police question you –'

'Which they will, but I don't want them doing so yet. I need you to find out what Steven has told them and stop him from saying too much. Can you keep the police off my back for a couple of days?'

'It won't be easy.'

'Tell them I'm working for you and I've had to go away on business.'

'Alex, what are you up to?'

'Probably best if you don't know.'

'If I'm being expected to lie for you, then don't you think I have a right to know. Don't you trust me?'

'It's not that,' I hastily interjected. Then paused. 'I'm not sure how to begin telling you. Look, I promise I'll tell you everything, just give me a day's breathing space.' I heard him thinking about it.

'OK. One day no more.'

That would do for now. On Monday I would be on that flight to Zurich. 'You can stay on the houseboat. There is one more thing. I need a bed for tonight and Sunday.'

Miles had a luxury apartment at Gun Wharf Quays overlooking Portsmouth harbour. I could go from there to the airport.

'I'll leave a set of keys with my neighbour,' Miles answered with a sigh.

'My solicitor is on his way,' I addressed Scarlett. 'He'll call the police station and tell them he's coming. Don't worry, Percy. It'll be all right.'

'I wish she'd never come here,' Percy uttered with bitterness. I knew he meant Deeta. I was inclined to agree with him. By her expression Scarlett thought so too.

'It's happening all over again, isn't it?' Percy mumbled.

Scarlett said, 'What is?'

'First Hugo, then Alex and now Steven.'

Scarlett looked baffled but something in Percy's words brought me up sharply. What if the old man was right? I had been fitted up. What if Steven and Hugo had also been framed?

'Percy, why did you say Hugo?'

'Leave him alone, Alex. Can't you see he's not well.'

'Why Hugo?' I pressed, ignoring Scarlett, thinking of those bones in the folly.

Percy looked frightened. I didn't want to be cruel but I knew that this was important. 'What really happened, Percy? I think it's time for the truth.'

'Alex!' Scarlett said sharply.

'No, Scarlett.' I turned to Percy. 'It wasn't Max who betrayed Hugo, was it?' Finally the truth was beginning to dawn on me.

Percy licked his lips and looked half scared to death.

'Was it?' I demanded harshly, ignoring Scarlett's glare.

The old man slumped. His body shrivelled in on itself. 'No. It was me.'

'Only you?' I eyed him carefully. 'The truth, Percy, please. It's important and it might help Steven.'

His eyes dropped. 'I heard Max tell your grandfather that he had seen Hugo signalling out to sea, to a German submarine, a few days before the Ventnor radar station was bombed. He said they had to tell the authorities that Hugo was a German spy.'

'Max knew you were hiding behind those rocks,' I said. 'He deliberately made you think Hugo was the traitor and you fell into his trap. You went straight to the authorities. That's why you were horrified when you discovered that Max was German. You realised you had betrayed the wrong man.'

Percy nodded slowly. His face was anguished. His bony hands were constantly wringing in his lap. There were tears in his eyes.

'My mother went to the authorities with you, didn't she?'

Percy nodded miserably.

'Then my grandfather went out on his boat and never returned.' Or rather he didn't. I guessed that my grandfather was lying in the folly he had built, killed and dumped there by Max Weber. Max had taken my father's boat to rendezvous with the German submarine, if it existed. Or he had used the boat to escape to the Channel Islands or France.

Scarlett said, 'Surely this can't be why you were framed, Alex?'

'I think it was. And I think that whoever did it is now framing Steven for Deeta's murder.'

'But who can it be?' she asked.

I turned to Percy. 'Was Hugo married? Did he have any children?'

Percy's breathing was becoming more laboured. Scarlett looked worried. The old man was clutching his chest.

'Call an ambulance, Scarlett,' I commanded, loosening Percy's shirt. 'It's OK, Percy. Take it easy. Everything will be all right.'

'Hugo ….was …. married,' he panted.

Ruby turned her attention from the television and said, 'What's wrong with him?'

'Percy, it's OK,' I insisted, growing more concerned as he clearly was in a great deal of pain.

'Amelia,' Percy whispered. 'Ask Amelia.'

'Who's Amelia?'

Percy gave a strangled cry and clutched his chest. His body twisted forward and slid to the floor before I could prevent it. He cried out again, writhing in pain. I was no doctor but I knew a heart attack when I saw one.

'The ambulance will be here in a moment. Steven will be fine. Take it easy,' I tried to reassure him.

I could hear Scarlett's muffled tones in the background. Percy gripped my hand and stared up at me with wild frightened eyes. He was mouthing something. I bent my head closer to his lips, feeling the gentle breath on my face as he struggled to talk, but there was no sound.

Then Ruby said quite lucidly, 'Amelia was Hugo's wife.'

Which meant that Hugo could have a grandson or grandaughter hell bent on revenge. And I had to find out who that was and quick.

Scarlett and Ruby followed the ambulance to the hospital. I hurried along to the Windmill Hotel praying that Deeta's father hadn't returned to Germany. He hadn't. I located him from Scarlett's description: a tall, rather distinguished-looking man with fair hair swept off an aquiline face, which was etched with sorrow. He looked very much like the older version of Max in the photograph that Ruby had taken.

I joined him in a quiet corner of the bar where he was staring into a glass of red wine. My heart went out to him. He had lost a daughter. I knew how I would feel if I lost one of my sons. Now, I was more determined than ever to get Andover and seek revenge not only for my lost years but for Deeta's too. It shouldn't have ended for her like that.

'Mr Weber?'

His head came up. I could hardly bear to see the pain in his eyes.

I told him I had been a friend of Deeta's and passed on my inadequate condolences. He could shed little light on his daughter's death but he confirmed what Percy had told me, that she had been strangled. As far as he knew there had been no diary, or photograph in her personal effects.

I said that Deeta and I had been brought together because of the friendship between Max and my grandfather.

'I know that Max was in England until August 1940. There doesn't seem to be any trace of him here after that date.'

'No. He went to Switzerland. He only returned to Germany after the war.'

I wondered if that was the truth.

'Max was Swiss German,' Deeta's father added. 'He spoke excellent English and he was educated at Cambridge.'

Which explained how he came to know Hugo and my grandfather.

'He wasn't a Nazi. He had no sympathy with Hitler. I've never been exactly sure what he did in the war, and he would never talk about it, but I believe he worked for the British Government.'

Had Max in fact been working for both sides? I didn't mention this, or the matter of Max creaming off money bringing Jews out of Germany. I thought Deeta's father had enough to cope with. It did however explain the fact that Max must have known his way around getting a Swiss bank account, which I guessed was where the three men had put the money from their exploits. My grandfather had taken his secret to his dusty grave in the folly, but what about Max's grandaughter and Hugo's descendants?

'Did Max leave any diaries or accounts of his past?'

Deeta's father shook his head. 'No. He might have spoken to Deeta about it before his death. I don't know. He worshipped her. I'm only glad he isn't alive now. This would have destroyed him.'

He looked sad and exhausted. My heart went out to him. I left a silence. I could hear the cars outside and some laughter from the adjoining restaurant. After a moment I asked, 'When did he die?'

'Three years ago.'

That surprised me. Why had Deeta waited until now to come in search of her grandfather's past? Had Max told her anything on his deathbed about his escapades with my grandfather and Hugo? Did she know about the Jews?

'Is your mother still alive?'

'No. She died ten years after they were married when I was nine. My father brought me up. Mr

Albury, what has this got to do with my daughter's death?'

'I don't know.' And I didn't, but there must be a connection.

Out of politeness I chatted with him a little longer about his daughter and his home in Bad Nauheim, then I left him to his sorrow and walked home mulling over what he had told me. If Max had told Deeta about his money gained from smuggling Jews out of Germany then why hadn't she claimed it? There were several answers to that question: Max had already spent it; Deeta was ignorant of it, or where the money was; or she didn't have all the information she needed to access it, which would explain her trip to the Isle of Wight, her questioning of Percy, her search of my houseboat and her eagerness to climb into bed with me, in case my grandfather had passed the secret on to me. Perhaps she had thought it was stashed away in the folly. Maybe it was. Scarlett and I had hardly searched it thoroughly. I thought it unlikely though.

But why did Deeta wait three years before coming here? The answer, of course, was quite simple. Me. Perhaps she had come here shortly after her grandfather had died only to find me in prison and my mother frail and forgetful. Perhaps Deeta had called on my mother before she had died. Of course, Deeta wasn't the only one interested in the missing money from the Jews. What of Hugo's grandson? It had to be a man because Ruby had seen a man push my mother down the stairs. She had thought it was Hugo, so the likeness must be significant. Hugo's grandson unable to find the information he was looking for in Bembridge House had perhaps threatened my mother, or had been surprised by her one day when he was in the house and had killed her. I'd make him pay for that. Had Deeta been working with him or alone?

Hastily I shut out the picture of my mother terrified. I needed a photograph of Hugo. Only Percy or Ruby would have one and I couldn't ask either of them. I had to risk returning to my houseboat. Besides I had to pack. I threw some things into a bag. There was no sign of the police.

Once again I delved into my mother's belongings, skimming quickly through the photographs trying to control my sorrow and feelings of guilt. Nothing. There were only a few and certainly no one I didn't recognise. I couldn't hang around waiting for Ruby and Scarlett to return in the vain hope that Ruby would have a photograph of Hugo. Time was running out. The police could show up at any minute.

A powerful sense of hopelessness clung to me during the forty-minute crossing of the Solent on the car ferry, and it was still there as I let myself into Miles's apartment. If Andover was a descendant of Hugo, and had wanted revenge for my mother betraying Hugo, did he know about the money from the Jews? Was that why he had used me as a scapegoat to swindle Westnam, Couldner and Brookes out of three million pounds: a sum he thought he was entitled to? But how had Hugo's descendant discovered that it was my mother and Percy who had betrayed his grandfather? Percy hadn't told him and neither had my mother.

I called Gus. He didn't answer immediately and when he did he sounded exhausted. I understood how emotional strain drained you more than physical effort.

I told him about the plans I'd made with Rowde.

'But you don't have the money, Alex.'

'Rowde doesn't know that. As soon as we've taken off call the Specialist Investigations Unit and ask for Detective Chief Inspector Crowder. Tell him everything. He'll know what you're talking about. You got that?'

'Yes. I could fly you there.'

'No. I don't want you mixed up in this. And I need you to be this end to see that Vanessa and the boys are safe.'

After a moment he agreed.

'In case I don't come back look after my sons.' My voice faltered. Gus took a deep breath before he said:

'Good luck.'

'I'll need it.' I rang off. Almost immediately my phone rang. It was Miles.

'I've left Steven at the hospital by his father's side. It doesn't look too good for the old man.'

I felt sad for Percy and sorry for Steven.

Miles said, 'The police will call me when they're ready to resume questioning, but Steven had already told them about you and Deeta. They want to question you.'

'They can't, Miles. I've got to stay free,' I said desperately. And I told him about Rowde.

'Bloody hell! And Gus?'

'I've told him to lie low. He'll alert the police as soon as we're in the air.'

'And you and Rowde?'

'One of us might come back. If it's me, I'll need a good lawyer.'

There was silence.

I continued. 'You mustn't breathe a word of this to the police, Miles.'

'They might be able to help you find them.'

'That's only the half of it.' I told him about Westnam's body being dumped on my houseboat, and that I had slept with Deeta the night before she was killed. He listened in silence. He was probably thinking how on earth he could defend me this time.

When I had finished he said: 'You think Andover killed Deeta?'

'Yes. To frame Steven this time, not me.'

'Why?'

'That's another long story. I'll tell you about it one day.'

'Alex, do you know who Andover is?'

'I thought it was Gus. He was having an affair with Vanessa at the time. I thought he wanted Vanessa for himself and so set out to destroy my reputation in order to get her. Now I think it might have something to do with what happened in the war.'

'Which one?' Miles asked surprised.

'The Second World War.'

Miles scoffed. I didn't blame him.

'I told you it was a long story. How safe am I in your apartment from the police?'

'Safe enough.'

'The police know you're my lawyer and my friend, won't they make the connection?'

'They haven't asked me if I know where you are, and when they do I'll tell them I haven't got a clue. They can't search my apartment without a warrant, or without asking me. They know that if they do, being a lawyer, I'll have them by the balls.'

I didn't feel entirely comfortable about it but Miles had a point. 'Is Steven all right alone? The police won't try to trap him into saying anything whilst he's vulnerable, will they?'

'With Scarlett beside him? She's quite a girl.'

She was. God alone knew what she thought of me. I hoped it wasn't too awful. Her opinion of me mattered. It shouldn't have done, but it did.

I rang off and stared across the narrow strip of water of Portsmouth Harbour to the lights twinkling in the town of Gosport opposite. Where was Rowde keeping Vanessa and the boys? I assumed here on the mainland but what if they were on the Island?

I moved away from the window and began to pace the living room. To get to the Island they would either have crossed on the ferry, too risky for Rowde, or been taken across by private yacht. Did Rowde have a yacht? The first time I saw him he looked as if he had just stepped off a luxury cruiser. Could they have come across on someone else's boat? Rowde wasn't a sailor as far as I knew and wouldn't know anything about crossing the Solent, and I doubted if marble man could skipper a boat. So who could have taken them? No, they had to be here on the mainland.

I needed a drink. I opened one of Miles's kitchen cabinets and began searching for something alcoholic that might numb my senses for a while and let me sleep, albeit fitfully. Miles wasn't the tidiest of men. Things were stashed in any old how. There was nothing in the kitchen. Perhaps I would find something in the lounge. I retrieved a bottle of Glenfiddich from a sideboard, and as I did a folder fell out. It was stashed full of photographs. I poured myself a drink and went to replace the folder in the cupboard when a couple of snapshots caught my eye. They were of a Hardy 50 motorboat and Miles was on the deck. I was surprised. I didn't know he owned a boat. He'd never said, but then there was quite a lot I didn't know about Miles.

As I sipped my drink I recalled our conversations over the years; they had all been about me, obviously. I knew Miles was single, hard-working, and a partner in a thriving law practice in Portsmouth. And that, I realised, was about the sum total of it.

I sat back thoughtfully, nursing my drink and staring at the photograph. It was the type of boat that could easily have taken Vanessa and the boys to the Isle of Wight. In fact it was the type of boat that could have taken them to the Channel Islands, to France or anywhere around the world.

I tossed back the whisky and rose, irritated with myself. I had no reason to think they had been transferred to a boat. They could be imprisoned in a country cottage, a council house, or a caravan for all I knew.

I pushed the folder back inside the cupboard. It got stuck on something. Annoyed I reached in and as I did I dropped the folder.

'Damn!' I scooped up the snapshots until my hand froze. I was staring at a very old and very small photograph, no bigger than two inches square. With a start I recognised instantly where it had been taken: in the background was my grandfather's folly. My pulse began to race. I could hardly believe what I was seeing. Why would Miles have a picture of the folly in his apartment? I took a breath and studied the two people in the photograph. The man was about thirty, rather short, square with piercing eyes and a wide smile and beside him was a young, fair-haired woman.

With shaking hands I turned the photograph over. There was nothing written on the reverse, but that didn't matter because I knew who I was staring at. It was Hugo and Amelia Wildern. And I also knew, without any doubt, who Hugo's grandson was: Miles Wolverton.

# CHAPTER 16

I stuffed the photograph in my pocket, grabbed my bag and caught the ten o'clock car ferry back to Fishbourne. The scope of Miles's betrayal was breathtaking. As I sat on the ferry recalling the last few years of my life I found his duplicity hard to comprehend. He had seemed so genuine. He had defended me with such vigour. He had always been there for me, telephoned me and visited me in prison. It had all been an act. How he must have gloated and silently crowed at my downfall. He had robbed me of everything. The bastard!

Now I had confessed to him that I had found Westnam's body and he knew about Deeta; yet more ammunition to humiliate me further. I wasn't going to call and alert him. I wanted to have this out with him face to face. But I'd bide my time. First I needed to know if he had a house on the Island, which must be where he was keeping Vanessa and the boys. It made sense. Now all I had to do was find it.

There was one person who might know: the cleaning lady Miles had engaged to clean my houseboat, Angela. I tried Scarlett's number several times. Her mobile was switched off. I guessed she was still at the hospital. Just after I disembarked I tried her again. This time she answered. I let out a sigh of relief.

'I've just left Steven alone with Percy for a while and stepped outside,' she said.

I was surprised that I had room to feel a stab of sorrow in my rapidly hardening heart.

'Scarlett, this is important. The lady who cleaned my houseboat for me, before I came out of prison, do you know her?'

'Angela? Yes, I work with her at the hotel. Why?'

'I'll explain when I see you. Do you know where she lives?'

'What is this, Alex?'

'Just tell me, Scarlett,' I said urgently.

'Victoria Lane, Nettlestone. Number twenty-four –'

I cut her off. As I drove through the wet night I considered the facts again. If my family were on the Island and Rowde had brought them here, then he was in league with Miles. Rowde had known about the three million pounds when we had been in prison together, but how had he known where to find Westnam? And where to find me? Miles had obviously told him. Gus's words came back to me. *'He knows every move you make almost before you make it.'* Of course he did. I told him.

Miles knew when I was being released. Miles knew scumbags like Rowde. Miles knew I had been going to see Joe on the morning he was killed. And I guessed that Miles had asked Joe to give him the reports on my investigation and had then extracted certain pieces of information from them before passing them on to me when I was in prison. Miles had got the press cuttings for me, and had the opportunity to remove those he didn't want me to see. What an idiot I had been not to see it before.

I located the small terraced house and was relieved to find a light still on. Angela eyed me warily and kept me standing on the doorstep. Behind her was a burly man with a full beard, glowering at me, her husband I guessed, who was ready to defend his wife, or call the police, if I threatened trouble.

I hastily apologised for the lateness of my visit and said, 'I need to know why Mr Wolverton asked you to clean for me. It's urgent and I can't really explain now? How do you know him? Has he got a house here on the Island?'

She looked at me with a mixture of surprise and suspicion. 'I don't know. I haven't cleaned for him before.'

Damn. I was wrong. I couldn't be. 'So why did he ask you?' I repeated as patiently as I could.

'I was recommended.'

'By whom?'

'Scarlett.'

'Scarlett!' I couldn't keep the surprise from my voice. How did she know Miles? She couldn't be part of this surely?

Angela said, 'Scarlett told me that Mr Wolverton was looking for someone to clean your houseboat before you – came home.'

'Why didn't she do it herself?'

Angela shrugged. 'I don't know. Didn't want to, I suppose.' She was closing the door on me as she spoke and I let her.

Why hadn't Scarlett told me that she'd recommended Angela when I'd telephoned her earlier? Was she hiding something? Was she involved in this? My stomach churned at the thought. I had trusted to her. I liked her; no, it was more than that.

I drove to the hospital, where I found her sitting in a small waiting room with Ruby.

'Percy died a few minutes ago,' she said. Her eyes were red where she had been crying. Surely she couldn't have deceived me! She couldn't be in league with Miles. I remembered her dishevelled appearance when she'd answered the door to me once, when Ruby had been at the day centre and I'd just returned from hospital. I had thought she was with a man then. Could it have been Miles? I felt sick at the thought.

She said, 'Steven's still with him. I shall drive him home when he's ready to go. Your lawyer friend wasn't much good. He couldn't get away quick enough.'

'Has he got a house on the Island?'

She stared at me in surprise. 'How the hell should I know?'

Was she telling me the truth? Perhaps he was keeping them on his boat. Was it moored up at Bembridge or Cowes? Christ, I was clutching at straws! Miles might not have anything to do with their kidnap. But Miles *was* Hugo's grandson, which meant he had to be Andover.

It was clear by Scarlett's expression that she didn't much like Miles. Was it an act or genuine? I didn't know who I could trust anymore.

'Why did you recommend Angela to clean my houseboat,' I asked as calmly as I could whilst my mind was racing and my heart pounding fit to burst.

Scarlett looked exasperated. 'What is all this about Angela?'

'Did you know Miles before I came out of prison.' I watched her closely for a reaction.

'Didn't you hear me say Percy's just died. Is that all you can think about, who cleaned your sodding houseboat?'

'Scarlett, my family are being held hostage. Just tell me the bloody truth, how deep are you in all this?'

'All what?' she blazed, her face flushing. 'You think I could hurt your family? You think I'm a crook like my dad was? Bugger off, Alex.' She turned away from me. I grabbed her arm.

'Gladly, but not until you tell me truth.'

'Truth! What is the goddamn truth? That my mother's dying before my eyes, my father in-law's just died of a heart attack brought on because of the truth of what happened nearly seventy years ago, and my ex-husband's been arrested for murder because he told the truth about following Deeta. The truth is that I'm scrimping and slaving away in a menial job to make enough money to keep myself and my mother alive.' Tears sprang to her eyes. 'The truth is that life stinks and so do you.'

'Scarlett, I'm desperate –'

'And what do you think I am?' Suddenly though her sorrow overcame her anger. Her body slumped. In a flat voice she said, 'I saw your lawyer friend at the airfield one morning. I'd gone to talk to Steven about something. Steven introduced me –

'Steven knows Miles!' Now I was surprised.

'Yes. He regularly flies into Bembridge. I didn't know that of course. Steven's only just told me. He didn't realise it would be Miles who would turn up to represent him. Your lawyer friend asked me if I knew any cleaners. He told me you were coming out of prison and your houseboat needed cleaning.'

I reeled with what Scarlett was telling me. Miles had a pilot's licence! I saw in my mind's eye his hand waving from the window of his car as he headed towards St Helen's on the day of my release. Of course, how easy for him to double back, follow me, and see me take the path across the airfield to Brading. All he had to do was climb into an aeroplane and watch for my return. Or perhaps he had been working with Deeta and she had called him to say I was leaving Brading Church. And it wasn't a boat that had brought my family here, but an aeroplane. Miles had flown them into Bembridge. Where would he have taken them? It explained how Steven knew about my release from prison.

Scarlett said, 'I didn't want him to know I was a cleaner. It was my stupid pride. I gave him Angela's name. She cleans for the London lot that invade Seagrove Bay in the summer months.'

Just then Steven entered. Scarlett turned her back on me. 'Are you ready to go home?'

He nodded. His face was ashen and there were dark circles under his dull, sad eyes. 'The police want me to report to them tomorrow.' He addressed his remark to me. 'They think I killed her.'

'Have they charged you?'

'Not yet. I told them I would call into the station tomorrow with Mr Wolverton.'

'Steven, did Miles Wolverton fly in here yesterday with a woman and two boys, one dark haired, the other fair,' I asked impatiently.

Scarlett glowered at me. Steven looked dazed. 'No.'

I cursed.

'But I think that was Miles Wolverton flying the day you said that aeroplane buzzed you,' he added.

Miles *was* Andover. I was in the corridor when Scarlett called after me.

'I can't stop now,' I shouted back.

'You might like to know your friend Ray called.'

I'd almost forgotten about him. That was quick. I halted. 'And?'

'He said it's drugs and it's not Jamie but Joanne. She nearly got done six years ago but got off the charge. Some clever bugger lawyer were his words. Fits your friend quite nicely, don't you think?'

Oh, indeed it did. I rushed towards her, took her face in my hands and kissed her. Before she could respond I had gone. Westnam, Couldner and Brookes – all with a secret they didn't want exposed. Who would they have told their secrets too? Who could they have trusted? There were only two answers to that question: a priest and a clever bugger lawyer. If I needed confirmation that Miles was Andover this was it. But knowing it didn't mean I knew where my family was, or that I would get them safely away from Rowde's clutches. I did know where Miles was though.

I drove through the empty streets as fast as I could praying there were no traffic cops about.

When I reached the curve in Embankment Road I saw his car. Parking behind it I climbed out, my fists clenched, my body rigid with anger. At last I was going to meet Andover face to face. Finally I was going to learn the truth. With a quickening heartbeat I pushed back the door of my houseboat and stepped inside.

# CHAPTER 17

Spread out before Miles were my mother's diaries and jewellery. He looked up surprised, then smiled warily. My instinct was to rush at him and beat the truth from him, but I wasn't certain I would be able to stop myself from killing him. With difficulty I controlled my raging anger. There were questions that I needed answers to first. Like where were my family?

'You won't find what you're looking for there,' I said, tautly.

'What? Oh sorry, didn't mean to pry. I was curious. It was rude of me.' His green eyes were scrutinising me. 'What are you doing back here?'

He was still trying to be friendly. He hadn't yet worked out that I knew. Time to enlighten him.

'I reckoned that Rowde had Vanessa and the boys on the Island. Where are they, Miles?' I crossed to stand opposite him.

'How should I know?' He pulled himself up to face me.

'Because you asked Rowde to kidnap them.'

His surprise was so genuine that I doubted myself. Then I told myself that Miles was a consummate actor. He had to be to have fooled the courts, the police and me all these years.

'Why did you frame me? Is it really because my mother betrayed your grandfather? Seems a bit ridiculous to me.' I spoke with what I hoped was calculated contempt. I saw just a flicker of anger flash in his eyes. He made to speak, then decided against it.

'You also killed Deeta so that Steven could be accused of murder. You got your own back on Percy too. He's dead by the way. You're Andover, Miles, and you framed me for something that happened to your grandfather almost seventy years ago. For the sake of revenge you killed my mother and stripped me of everything I owned and loved. You destroyed my life.' My fists clenched. The blood pounded in my head. I willed myself not to strike him. It took every ounce of self-control I possessed.

Miles looked as though he was about to deny it. If he did I knew I wouldn't be able to contain myself any longer.

He said, 'How did you find out?'

'Joanne Brookes, drug smuggling charge, some clever bugger lawyer got her off.'

'And you've put it all together from that?'

'And this.' I held out the photograph. 'Your grandfather, I believe: Hugo Wildern. I take it you killed Joe before I could get to him and you took my file from the warehouse?'

I could see him weighing it up: truth or more lies. In the end he saw he didn't really have a choice. He sat down. 'Your file didn't contain much but I couldn't take the risk. Joe gave me the reports, but I wasn't sure if he had kept copies. As it was, I needn't have bothered.'

Jesus! The arrogance of the man. 'And Darren? The man in the warehouse? Did you kill him?'

Miles didn't answer. He didn't have to; I could see that he had.

I said, 'I know Joanne Brookes was into drug smuggling at one time and that you managed to get the charges dropped but what about Westnam and Couldner? What were their secrets?'

I forced myself to sit opposite him and emulate his causal manner whilst my heart was screaming kill him, beat him to a pulp. My mind, however, was racing, wondering how this might get me to my family. Was Rowde working alone? I needed to find out and quickly. I could see though I wouldn't be able to hurry Miles.

'I suppose there's no harm in your knowing now. Westnam left a banker's dinner early. I was there. He was drunk. On his way home on a quiet country road he knocked over and badly injured a woman. He couldn't afford the scandal. He called me. I collected him and took him home to bed. I told the police that I had been talking to Westnam and that he and I had been together at the time of the incident. The car had been stolen and flashed up.'

'When it hadn't. And Couldner?'

'We were at a party at Couldner's managing director's house. Couldner got carried away with the MD's daughter. She was fifteen. He always did like them young. I told the girl that if she breathed a word about it, her father would be dismissed.'

I wanted to hit him hard. With difficulty I contained my fury and disgust. I couldn't afford to rattle him. Prison had trained me well. If Miles attacked me I guessed I could give as good as I got, but I wasn't going to take any chances yet. Not until Vanessa and my sons were safe. And if I couldn't find my family on time…? If Miles wouldn't tell me where they were…? Then I had to keep that meeting with Rowde.

Miles said, 'How did you find out about Joanne Brookes?'

'I've got contacts too, Miles. Who told you about your grandfather?'

'It was a coincidence really. Life is full of them. It makes you wonder, doesn't it? I think it was meant to be. I saw it as justice. Fate had put it within my grasp and I couldn't ignore it, Alex.'

'You'll be telling me you hear voices next.'

Miles lips twitched but his eyes glared. Why hadn't I seen before how mad he was? The answer was because he had defended me with passion and vigour, because he was my friend. My only friend, after all the others faded away. And I had needed a friend so badly.

Miles said, 'I was defending the usual thug on a charge of manslaughter. It was about fifteen years ago. His grandfather was in court and he came up to me after I got his beloved grandson off. He said, "You must be related to Hugo Wildern. I'll never forget him. You look so alike." I told him he must be mistaken. My grandfather's name was Baxter. But when my mother died about two months after that I was going through her papers and I found a letter from Amelia, my grandmother, to Hugo.

'I found the old man and asked him what he knew of Hugo. He told me he'd been in the prison service during the war when Hugo had been arrested for treason in 1940. He said that Hugo always maintained he was not a German spy but nobody believed him. Hugo told him that he had been helping Jews get out of Germany for money and that a man called Max had betrayed him and that *he* was the German spy. One of the warders was a terrible bully, he regularly beat Hugo.'

Miles expression darkened and his body tensed.

'Hugo offered them the proceeds of his ventures if they would just stop hitting him but it didn't do any good. My grandfather was beaten to death and then his death covered up, forgotten, swept away, where's the justice in that?'

'There isn't any. But where was the justice in what you did to me? You killed my mother for God's sake!' I sprang up unable to sit mildly by and listen to his drivel. My body was poised for attack. 'You took away my life, my wife, my children, everything I held dear and valued.'

'She betrayed me,' he said evenly.

'No, she didn't,' I shouted. 'She betrayed your grandfather, Miles. Even then she was just a kid. Max put the idea into her and Percy's head.'

'And I decided their children should suffer for it as I had suffered.'

'You! How have you suffered? You've got a good job, plenty of money.'

'It's not enough, is it, Alex, as you found out. It's nothing without your reputation.'

I stared at him. Incredibly through my anger and my sorrow I saw that he was right. Through the turmoil of my emotions I understood his warped reasoning.

Miles continued. 'When I knew the truth of my grandfather's betrayal I came looking for Percy. I found his son Steven Trentham in a terrible state after being shot down in the Gulf War. He'd had some kind of breakdown. His career was at an end and I didn't think the fiery Scarlett would hang around him for long, rightly as it turned out. I thought he's had his punishment, so I turned to Olivia Albury and found you.'

His voice harsher now he continued. 'Alex Albury: a very successful businessman, wealthy, beautiful family, attractive loving wife, large expensive house, a yacht. You had the perfect life. Not only that but you stood to inherit Bembridge House. Because of my grandfather's fate, brought on by your mother, my grandmother had lived a life of shame and hardship, struggling to raise her daughter, my mother. My mother married a dockyard worker in Portsmouth. Fortunately I was clever and won a scholarship to the grammar school, then university and law school. But there was no money. At least that was what I thought until the old man told me about the Jewish money. The three million pounds from Westnam, Couldner and Brookes is peanuts compared to that.'

'You know the amount?' I asked surprised.

'I'm guessing, but I know where it is. My mother left me this.'

He reached into his pocket and drew out a cameo brooch. It looked vaguely familiar. I was sure my mother had worn one very similar. Then it came to me. She had been wearing it in the photograph that Deeta had taken from me.

Miles turned the brooch over to reveal a number engraved on the reverse. He said, 'I knew at once that the money must be in a Swiss bank account and that this was only part of the number. I had to find the other two brooches. What had happened to Edward Hardley's? Had he passed it down to his daughter, Olivia? Or had it gone down with him on his boat when he drowned?'

Or, I thought, was it rotting with his bones in the folly? But it couldn't have been if my mother had been wearing it in that photograph of me with the telescope. That had been taken a long time after my grandfather's death.

Miles said, 'With you in prison I could search your mother's house. It wasn't there. I asked her, but she wouldn't say.'

I leapt forward to strike him but he was quicker. His punch came before I could even see it, right in my stomach. I buckled over, winded.

'She did fall. I didn't push her.'

I didn't believe him. I vowed silently I would kill him for that.

He said, 'It's not here with your mother's jewellery, so where is it, Alex?'

'Were you working with Deeta?' I panted, trying to recover my breath.

'Yes. I discovered who she was from Steven Trentham. I approached her and we joined forces to find the third brooch, yours. When I knew you were heading across the marshes to Brading the morning you were released I told her to make contact with you. If I couldn't find the brooch then I guessed she might be able to get the information from you, after all a beautiful girl like her, and you a man who'd spent years in prison…'

'But all she discovered was the photograph,' I snarled.

'Yes.' Miles unfurled his hand and now there were two brooches. 'I just need yours for the hat trick.'

'You killed her for that.'

'Yes. Where, is it, Alex?' He clenched his fist ready to strike me again.

'Get stuffed.'

His fist came out, but before he had a chance to hit me the door flew open and in tumbled a bedraggled and very wet Ruby.

'Hugo!' she cried, staring at Miles. Fear swiftly chased away the surprise on his face. Of course, she'd seen him bring me home from prison and again leaving my houseboat. It was why she had confused me with Hugo on our first encounter.

'She's old and she's got Alzheimer's,' I said quickly, afraid for Ruby's safety. Miles wouldn't spare her. 'She won't remember and no one will believe her even if she did say anything.'

'Not good enough.'

I saw him smile at her. She returned it.

'I always knew you'd come back,' Ruby said. 'I told Livvy you would. She said she'd seen you, but I didn't believe her. I knew you wouldn't visit her and not me. I was always your favourite, wasn't I?'

'Of course you were.'

Miles took hold of her bony arm. She was soaking wet. Her pink summer dress was almost purple as it clung to her and the gloves grasping her handbag were sodden. Her sparse grey hair was plastered to her scalp. Where was Scarlett? Did she know her mother was out? Would she come here looking for her? God, I hoped not.

'Give me the brooch, Alex,' Miles said, his voice heavy with menace.

'I haven't got it.' It was the truth. It certainly hadn't been in with my mother's jewellery that I'd collected from the solicitor. Perhaps it had been thrown out when my mother died? Perhaps Vanessa had it.

'Wrong answer.'

Miles had Ruby by the neck before I could even raise a fist. His great big hand was squeezing her throat so that her eyes bulged.

'Let her go!' I cried

'That's up to you.'

Ruby was making choking noises.

'I haven't got it,' I yelled.

'You're lying.'

He tightened his grip on Ruby. Her body was going limp. I had to do something.

'I'll get it for you,' I cried, quickly thinking.

'When?'

'Monday. Kerry, the solicitor's, got it,' I lied.

Miles relaxed his hold a little on Ruby's throat. The fear in her eyes tore at my heart.

'Just let her go. She won't tell anyone and on Monday I'll get the brooch. In return let Vanessa and the boys go free. You can have the money, Miles, and welcome to it.'

'You're bluffing.'

I was, but he couldn't know that. How could I have trusted this man? What a fool I had been. Then an idea came to me. Just as it had with Rowde, I was playing this wrong.

'OK, if that's what you think, have it your own way. If you are prepared to let my boys die, then there is no point in me living. It's no go, Miles. No brooch.'

'Then she dies.'

I shrugged. 'Please yourself. She means nothing to me. She's old and she's got Alzheimer's. You'd be doing her a favour.' Think 'prison' I urged myself. Practice what you'd been taught.

There was silence. In it I could hear the sea washing against the boat and the wind as it roared and whistled around us. I held his gaze. After a moment he sighed and released Ruby.

She coughed. Her crying was like a soft whimper. A mixture of bewilderment and fear was in her eyes. I crossed to her.

'On Monday the brooch will be yours.' I held Miles eyes. 'But I can only get it if you call off Rowde. I'm meant to be going to Zurich with him. Let Vanessa and the boys go.'

'He'll want the three million.'

'Then for Christ's sake tell him where it is. According to you it's nothing compared to what Hugo, Max and Edward took from the Jews. Take the bloody brooches and claim what you think is your compensation for your grandfather's betrayal.'

I could see him thinking about it. I held my breath praying for him to agree.

'OK.'

I didn't trust him. He would betray me. He would leave me to face Rowde. As long as I could get Vanessa and the boys to safety before then I didn't care. As soon as they were out of Rowde's clutches I would go to the police and tell them everything. I would get protection from Rowde and they would arrest Miles.

I put my arm around Ruby and tried to steer her towards the door but she must have thought I was going to hurt her. She struggled against me. Then breaking free, she screamed and ran outside. I cursed. I couldn't let her go in that state. I rushed out after her.

At the bottom of the gangway she stumbled and fell onto the shingle below. I hurried towards her and leant over to pull her up. The rain was lashing against us. She was sobbing and filthy. She was skin and bone and trembling from head to foot. I put my arm around her, but she was screaming something, which I finally realised was: 'My handbag! Where's my handbag?'

'Here it is,' Miles said.

Something in his voice made me stiffen. I turned. The bag was open and so was his left hand. I saw what was in it. It was the third brooch.

# Chapter 18

'That's mine,' Ruby cried. 'Livvy gave it to me.'

'Livvy's not around anymore. She would have wanted Hugo to have it,' Miles wheedled.

Ruby's face puckered up as though she was trying to recall something.

'For God's sake, Miles, take the wretched thing and let me get her into the warm,' I pleaded with him.

'No. She knows too much and so do you. Move.'

He dropped the handbag and now I saw with horror what had replaced it. He was holding a revolver and it was pointing right at us.

'It comes in handy knowing the criminal fraternity when you want something useful like this.' He indicated the gun.

'Miles, you can't do this.' I roared.

'Move. Round to the back of the houseboat.'

My heart was pounding. My mind racing. Was he going to shoot us there?

'This is crazy,' I tossed over my shoulder, the wind catching my words and carrying them into the black night. I was half carrying and half shoving Ruby and by now we were ankle deep in water. The cold took my breath away; God knew how Ruby felt. She was crying and trembling, leaning heavily against me. I could see that she was on the point of collapse. 'You've got the brooches, go and get the fucking money.'

'Gladly, I just need to tidy up a couple of loose ends. Get in the boat,' he commanded.

I made to protest but saw there was little point. I climbed in and then helped a whimpering Ruby in.

'Start it up.'

I did as I was told. The engine refused to start on the first couple of tries. Perhaps if it didn't work he might let us go, I thought in desperation.

Then the damn thing spluttered into life and was merrily chugging away.

'Let's go for a nice little sea journey.'

'In this storm? You must be mad.'

'I don't think so.' He slipped the line that was attached to my houseboat. 'Out or I kill the old woman now.'

I knew he was going to kill her anyway, and me, but if I did as he asked it would buy me time to think of a way out of this. The tide was carrying us with it. It was dark and I had to navigate my way through the buoys, just as I had done with Westnam in the boat.

'Did you kill Westnam?' I shouted above the wind.

'No.'

It must have been Rowde then. I prayed that we might be spotted from another boat. But on a night such as this, who would be daft enough to be on their boat? And even if they were they would certainly be down below.

'Don't worry, Alex, I've got it all worked out,' Miles sneered. 'You killed Ruby because she saw you follow Deeta that morning. Then you killed yourself because you couldn't live with what you had done and you didn't want to go back to prison.'

'How will the police know that if I'm dead?'

We were reaching the end of the channel; soon we would be into the Solent and exposed.

'Because I will tell them,' shouted Miles above the wind and rain. 'You confessed to me, your lawyer.'

The gun was rammed right up against poor Ruby but she seemed not to notice. I think she was too far gone for that. None of us were wearing protective sailing clothes; my jeans and sweater were soaked so was Ruby's thin dress and cardigan and Miles suit. This was madness.

'We can't go any further,' I shouted with difficulty against the roar of the wind and sea. 'We'll all be killed.' The waves were crashing over us. For the first time I thought Miles looked worried. 'I have to turn back or we'll all be drowned.'

'Keep going,' Miles commanded, stabbing Ruby with the gun. She had stopped crying but was crumpled in the cockpit. I could see her shivering uncontrollably. I was cold and wet, and if I didn't get her out of this soon she'd die from hypothermia.

Could I overpower him? Would I stand a chance? Could I jump him before he shot Ruby and take him into the sea with me? But what would happen to Ruby? And at this time of year we'd only last a few minutes in the freezing cold water. We were going further, heading around the coast towards the lifeboat station. The sea was so rough that it was like being on a big dipper in the funfair, only wet and not nearly so much fun. I stared at the gun: would it still work if it were wet?

Miles shouted, 'Keep going.'

He eyed Ruby. I could see that he was working out another way to kill her. I knew that all he had to do was push her over the side. Then he'd tackle me. I could put up a fight but Ruby would be gone.

'I have to turn back.' The wind snatched at my words and tossed them into the Solent. I knew it was too late. I couldn't see over the waves, we were riding them high then plunging into the troughs, the sea washing over us. At any minute a wave could and probably would hit us and take us down with it. I felt behind me. Somewhere there were a couple of flares, kept purposely near the helmsman in case of emergency. This was one all right. I could and should be able to lay my hands on one in the dark. I had to wait for Miles to look away, but I couldn't wait forever. Then as a particularly nasty wave bashed into us and Ruby slid down onto the deck my fingers curled around it. I didn't know if it would work but it was worth a try. If I didn't do something we were all going to die. If I tried we might have a chance. Then suddenly the air was filled with a loud bang as the lifeboat was launched, and I could no longer afford to hesitate.

I wrenched out my hand, pointed the flare directly at Miles, pulled Ruby towards me and shot the flare as Ruby and I went over the side of the boat together. A bright white light lit the sky. I thought I heard Miles cry out. The icy sea sucked the breath from my body. I struggled to hold Ruby above the tumultuous waves; her body was limp and weighed a ton. I concentrated on staying alive, trying to forget the mind numbing cold, the heavy clothes that were pulling me down, the salt that was swilling into my mouth and filling my lungs.

I was losing my grip on Ruby. I couldn't hold onto her any longer. She was slipping away. I was so cold. I could see David and Philip's laughing faces before me; I could hear them speaking, see them running along the beach, chatting on the boat with me on a bright summer's day. My mother was smiling at me, her arms were open and a white light was all around her. I was no longer cold; I was floating peacefully to that white light. It was over. Then strong hands were pulling me back, my mother was fading, the light had gone, something was being tied around me and I was being lifted out of the water.

'Ruby, ' I managed to choke.

I heard someone say, 'It's all right. We've got her.'

# CHAPTER 19

Hospital was the last place I could afford to go. Too many questions: like what was I doing in a boat in the middle of a stormy night with an elderly lady? I was the one with the criminal record, not Miles. I alone had heard Miles's confession. In DCI Crowder's eyes I was still James Andover. How was I ever going to prove my innocence now with Miles dead? And I was sure he was dead. No one could survive taking a flare full on. I had killed him in self-defence, but by the time I explained that (if they let me) it would be too late to meet Rowde. And meet him I had too because I still didn't know where Vanessa and my sons were being kept.

In the general commotion of getting Ruby into an ambulance and Miles's body from the sea I was able to duck into the darkness of Beach House Lane and, shivering in the silver thermal blanket the ambulance man had draped around me, I found a footpath that led back onto the beach and stumbled my way around the shore until I came to the Embankment. No one came after me. My adrenalin and my desperation were keeping me warm and propelling me forward.

There was no sign of life around my houseboat or Scarlett's. Scarlett's car had gone and I guessed that she was on her way to the hospital. I hoped Ruby was all right, but I wasn't betting on it.

A steaming hot shower, a shot of whisky and clean dry clothes and I was once again shutting the door behind me. Armed with a powerful torch I climbed into my car and headed for Steven's house. There was a light on. It was 2am. Steven answered the door. He didn't seem surprised to see me, but then I guessed he was in a state of shock and that numbness that follows bereavement.

I followed him through to the living room. He looked awful. I was no picture either I thought, catching a glimpse of myself in the mirror over the tiled fireplace.

'You said that Miles used to fly into Bembridge regularly. Do you know where he went when he came here?' I felt as though this was my last chance. Miles had to have a holiday home on the Island, otherwise why else would he come here so often? And I was convinced that must be where he was holding Vanessa and my sons.

Steven didn't answer me. 'Please, Steven, this is important to me. Miles is the person who framed me. He's holding my family hostage and he killed Deeta.'

My words finally penetrated Steven's sorrow. 'It was him? The murdering bastard. I'll kill him for that and for what he's done to my father.'

'You're too late. I've done the job for you.'

I sat down heavily. I would have to keep my rendezvous with Rowde. I just hoped he didn't learn of Miles's death before then. I would kill Rowde or be killed. I was coming to the end.

'I felt sure he flew them here, Vanessa and the boys,' I muttered.

'A woman and two boys did fly in but they weren't with Mr Wolverton,' Steven said.

My head shot up. My heart leapt into my throat. I could hardly dare to hope. Miles had got someone else to do his dirty work, unless Rowde could fly an aeroplane, which I doubted.

'A small dark-haired woman about forty?' I asked, eagerly.

'Mrs Newberry, yes.'

'You know her?' I said, surprised.

'Of course, she and Mr Newberry have a house on the Island. That's why they fly here –'

'Who flew them in?'

'Mr Newberry, of course…'

Gus! He'd brought them here? I sat up amazed and confused. Steven must have got it wrong.

'When was this?' I asked.

'Yesterday morning.'

That shook me. It was the day after Gus and I had returned from Guernsey. After he had shown me the note to say that Rowde had taken them. It wasn't possible. Steven must be mistaken. Grief had made him confuse the weeks.

'Are you sure it was Gus Newberry?' I persisted.

'Positive.'

I held Steven's eyes. He didn't seem confused. He wasn't lying either. Why should he be?

I ran a hand through my hair and stood up, trying desperately to make some sense of this. How could he be right? Vanessa and the boys had been kidnapped by Rowde. Gus had been distraught. There had been the note on the kitchen table. Then I remembered. He hadn't shown it to me. I hadn't seen what was written. Gus had picked it up and said, 'They're gone.' Of course they had gone, but not to the Isle of Wight. They must have been staying elsewhere, waiting for Gus to collect them and fly them here the following day. Which meant that Gus knew all along they hadn't been kidnapped. Gus must be in league with Rowde. Why? What did he want from me? Money? Did he really think I was Andover and he had used my family to get the three million from me? Was Gus in financial difficulty? How much did Vanessa know about this?

'Steven, where is Gus Newberry's house?' I asked, holding my breath, willing him to know.

'Gully Road, Seagrove Bay. It's new. Mr Newberry only bought it last year, a three storey house he told me.'

Steven barely noticed me leaving. I stared through the rain-spattered windscreen negotiating the dark, empty roads towards Seagrove Bay. Behind every deception there was yet another deception. I could hardly keep up with it, or comprehend it.

I turned into Gully Road and drove slowly down it. There were houses on the right hand side only. Towards the end, just before the bay, was a large detached three-storey house. It was in darkness. It was the early hours of Sunday morning. There was no sign of Rowde's car. I hadn't expected to see it. This must be Gus's house.

With a pounding heart I rang the bell. There was no answer. I rang again, this time keeping my finger on it. A light came on in the upstairs bedroom and then in the hall.

'Who is it?'

Relief flooded through me as I recognised the voice. 'Let me in, Vanessa.'

'Alex! Go away please.'

'Are David and Philip there?'

'Alex, this won't help.'

'Help what?' She didn't sound like a terrified kidnapped woman. But then why should she when she had come here with her husband? 'Do I have to shout at you through the door? I could wake the boys up. Do you want them asking questions?'

'You can't take them away from me, Alex.'

So that was it. 'Is that what Gus told you?'

'They're not going to live with you in Switzerland or anywhere else when you claim the money you stole. I'm not letting you take them. I'm calling the police.'

'You do that,' I said tautly. 'But first tell Gus what you're going to do.'

'What do you mean?'

'Is he there with you?'

'No.'

She was lying. 'Tell him I don't have the money.'

I left her. There was no Rowde or marble man here. There was no kidnap. Rowde had been paid by Gus to threaten me and Rowde had been conned into believing I really did have three million pounds. I didn't think he was going to be very happy when he discovered he'd been tricked. I didn't want to be the one to tell him, but it looked as though I might be. It was either that or confess everything to the police. I could just see Crowder's look of disbelief before he charged me with the murder of Westnam, Deeta and Miles. What was I going to do? I had to go back and confront Gus, and I had to do so in front of a witness, Vanessa.

I turned back, but had hardly gone two paces before a hand gripped my shoulder and spun me round. I was staring into the large, solemn face of DCI Crowder.

'You've been very busy, Alex. I think it's time we had a chat.'

My heart sank. This could only mean one thing: Crowder was about to arrest me. I had no choice but to fall into step beside him. I could hardly run away. I wouldn't get far. I could see the waiting car just ahead of us.

Crowder continued, 'You might like to know that a man's body has been washed up at Niton. What's left of his fingerprints matches those of Clive Westnam. Darren Cobden, the man in the storage warehouse where Joe kept your file, has also been found dead, on the tip at Port Solent in Portsmouth.'

This was worse than I had dared to imagine. I had forgotten about poor Darren, his chocolate covered little girl and his harridan of a mother.

'Quite a trail of murder and deception, wouldn't you say?' Crowder posed.

I snatched my head to look at him. 'I didn't kill any of them.'

'Not even Miles?'

'That was self-defence. He was going to kill Ruby Kingston and me.'

'And Westnam?'

'A thug called Rowde and his henchman are responsible for that. Miles killed Joe Bristow, Darren and Deeta. He was going to kill me.' I searched Crowder's face. It was devoid of expression. 'Please, you have to believe me,' I pleaded, seeing my freedom slip away.

'And have you discovered the identity of James Andover?' Crowder asked, quietly.

'It was Miles Wolverton.'

Christ, he still didn't believe me! My ex wife and sons might be safe, but I wasn't, not from arrest and not from Rowde.

'Get in the car, Alex.'

I did as I was told with a sinking heart. There had to be a way I could make Crowder believe me. Sergeant Adams started the engine and pulled away. Crowder swivelled to look at me. Suddenly I saw there was something different in his expression. I hardly dared to build my hopes up. Was it just possible he was prepared to listen to me, and to believe me?

'I –'

He held up a hand to staunch me. 'It's all right Alex, we know what Miles told you.'

I stared at him open mouthed. Then the light slowly dawned. I recalled the dark car with tinted windows parked on the slipway on my first day of freedom. Whilst I had gone for a walk a surveillance team had slipped in and planted a listening device. They'd *heard* Miles's confession. Relief washed over me, threatening to overwhelm me.

'You bugged the houseboat,' I said and stared out of the window trying to get my emotions under control. I was surprised to see that we were heading back towards St Helen's and not to Ryde and the police station. 'Where are we going?'

'I thought you might like a lift home.'

I was taken aback but didn't comment. Instead I said, 'You've been listening to everything, including me being beaten up by Rowde's thug. You even heard me making love to Deeta. Why didn't you tell the local force she was with me the morning she died?'

'Why should we? We know you didn't kill her.'

It took a moment to click, then I understood. 'You were following me.' I could have sworn that no one had been.

'Yes.'

My brain was beginning to function. 'You let me see that detective following me the morning of Joe's death. He was so obvious that I would believe I would be able to spot anyone else.' I'd even bragged to Rowde that I could spot and smell a copper. Well, I'd been wrong, thankfully. 'But why the interest? Did you really think I would lead you to the money?'

Crowder glanced at his watch. We were at the top of St Helen's. 'Pull over on the other side of the green,' he instructed the thin-faced sergeant. I stared at Crowder surprised, but he said nothing until we had stopped.

'DCI Clipton was coming to see you on the day of your release to tell you that he had got it wrong. He believed you to be innocent.'

'Not much good to me then,' I said with bitterness. 'Why did he tell his daughter he was going to see Andover if he thought me innocent?'

'Because he knew that Miles Wolverton was going to pick you up on your release from prison. I suppose he had some idea of confronting him with it in front of you. Clipton had called the prison; they told him that Miles was collecting you.'

'But how did he get to the conclusion that Miles was Andover?'

'We believe that he got suspicious when Roger Brookes committed suicide. We know that Brookes made a call to Clipton, but there was no record of what was said. Perhaps Brookes confessed before he killed himself, anyway it was enough to make Clipton act. He, like us, found out about Joanne Brookes and her drug smuggling. She was never charged though. Miles must have bribed someone high up to keep it quiet. We're still investigating that.'

'Did you find all this in his notebook and files when he was found dead in his car.'

'No, they *were* missing. Which is what got *us* thinking. Clipton was a stickler for writing things down. He would never go anywhere without his notebook. When we went to his house, after he died, we found some of his notebooks but not all of them.'

'Let me guess, the ones covering my questioning had vanished.'

'Yes, along with a couple of others but they were just decoys. When Christine Clipton told us about her father mentioning Andover we knew he must have been investigating you, and that he had discovered something important. We started from scratch, just like Clipton did, this time assuming you had been telling the truth.'

'Thanks,' I snarled. 'Did Clipton really die of a heart attack?'

'Yes. That was a stroke of luck for Miles Wolverton. Miles knew that Clipton was getting near to the truth; Joe Bristow had told him that Clipton had been asking questions about Joanne Brookes. Miles discovered from one of the prison warders that Clipton had called the prison to find out about the date and time of your release. Miles caught the same ferry and kept an eye on Clipton. He followed him down to his car when the ferry docked at Fishbourne. Then suddenly Clipton slumped against the steering wheel, Miles opened the back door and took Clipton's briefcase containing his mobile phone and notebooks.'

'It would have been nice if you had told me all this.'

'We didn't know much of it until the last twenty-four hours. We knew that you had made no secret that you would go after Andover. We thought you might lead us to him, and you did almost at the same time as we got there ourselves. We didn't know why you were the victim until we heard Miles tell you. We couldn't get to you in time before your boat trip, unfortunately. We were too far away.'

'How is Ruby?'

'She didn't make it. I'm sorry.'

And so was I. She hadn't deserved a death like that. And neither had my mother deserved to die. I was glad Miles had paid for both with his own life. I took a deep breath. Poor Scarlett. I didn't think she would ever forgive me for leading her mother to her death.

Crowder continued. 'Rowde's arrival on the scene complicated things and we were nearly persuaded to step in. Sorry you had to take a beating.'

'That makes me feel a lot better,' I said, sarcastically.

'You won't need to keep that appointment with Rowde by the way. We've picked him up and charged him and his henchman, Barry Chertsey, with extortion, wounding, oh and murder – Westnam's will do for a start.'

'I hope you've got enough evidence to put them away for a long time.'

'Rowde also told me that he was paid by Miles Wolverton to claim he had kidnapped your family.'

'I know. I've found them...' I faltered. Crowder's words jarred. Why? I urged my tired brain to function; it seemed intent on refusing to co-operate. Adams, at a sign from Crowder, began to head down into Port St Helens and the Embankment. Within a couple of minutes we pulled up outside my houseboat. I needed a drink and I needed to think. For that I needed to be alone. I couldn't get rid of them fast enough. Crowder didn't seem to mind. I promised I would make myself available later that morning, and watched them drive away.

Scarlett's car was in the lay-by opposite her houseboat and I could see a light in her window. My heart ached at the thought of her alone with her grief. I wanted to go to her, but how could I after what I had done?

I poured myself a stiff drink and took it to the patio doors. I pressed my forehead against the cold glass and urged myself to think. Crowder had said that Rowde had confessed that Miles Wolverton had paid him to say he had kidnapped Vanessa and the boys, but Gus had flown them here, and they were living in Gus's house. Gus had kidnapped them to make sure that Vanessa stayed afraid of me, and for the money he thought I had. Rowde was lying or was he?

I spun round. What a bloody fool I'd been. Why hadn't I seen it before? I could hardly believe it. Miles and Gus had been working together. Miles wasn't Andover. It was Gus and Crowder knew it. That was why he had asked me the question outright. It was why he had brought me back here. To wait for Andover to show up.

I tossed back the whisky, not tasting it, slammed the glass down on the table and paced the floor, my mind whirring trying to fit the pieces of the jigsaw together. I felt the breath being sucked from me as each piece slotted into place. As the incredible truth finally dawned on me, instead of the fury that I had felt confronting Miles, I was amazed to find myself quite calm. But it was a dangerous calm, full of hatred. At last I had come to the end of my journey. Or, rather I was near the end. There was one more confrontation to come. I knew it wouldn't be long before he came here. I snatched a glance at my watch and with immaculate timing my door was thrust open.

Gus was standing on the threshold.

# Chapter 20

At the sight of him the calmness inside me hardened with a resolve to see this man suffer, as I had suffered. I had already decided which way to play this. Physical violence wouldn't work. I'd learnt that much in Guernsey. No, with Gus I had to play to his superiority and his intellect.

'You look dreadful,' Gus said stepping inside and closing the door behind him.

'I'll live, which is more than you'll do when Rowde finds out you conned him.'

I could see him weighing things up. I needed Gus to think that Rowde was still free rather than in police custody.

'It's over, Gus. It's taken me a while, but I've finally got to the truth. Miles wasn't Andover. It was you.'

For a moment I thought he was going to deny it. Then vanity got the better of him. Hatred was in my soul for this man, but I also wanted justice and to *see* justice done. I was counting on the fact that Crowder hadn't yet removed his listening devices from the houseboat.

I said, 'Was it just Vanessa that you wanted from me, or did you also want the three million from your victims?'

'You tell me, Alex. You seem to have all the answers.'

'You set up the fake charity, you hacked into my computer and you sent those e-mails from my computer. Miles gave you your victims though: Couldner, Westnam and Brookes, three men with a secret that they were desperate to keep hidden. I suppose the idea for all of this came to you after you discovered that Miles was Hugo's grandson and that my mother and Percy Trentham had falsely betrayed Hugo. You went to Miles and told him and between you, you hatched up the plan to destroy my reputation and my marriage.'

I was amazed that I could keep my voice so even. It was as though I was discussing a business plan and not the ruination of my life, not to mention the destruction of my mother's life and now poor Ruby's. Oh, Miles had *killed* both women, but it was this man who had goaded him into doing it. To me he was the more evil of the two. I hated his smugness, his cleverness, his superiority. I could see even now, as I confronted him, he was arrogant enough to believe he could get away with it. I knew he wouldn't. What I had in mind for Gus Newberry wasn't a quick death like Miles's.

I went on. 'That story Miles told me about the elderly man recognising him in court was bullshit, wasn't it?'

Gus couldn't resist it, as I knew he wouldn't be able to. 'I admire you, Alex. I didn't think you'd get there, and if you did I felt sure you'd blame Miles.'

'Oh, I did until I discovered you had a house in Seagrove Bay and flew Vanessa and the boys here. I also know that Miles is hopeless with computers. He doesn't even have one on his office desk. The hi tech bit was beyond him. You bribed Rowde with a share of the three million pounds you and Miles extorted from Couldner, Westnam and Brookes.'

'You've got it all worked out.' Gus said evenly. 'Congratulations.'

I almost yielded then to the temptation of striking him. I willed myself to stay in control. I envisaged him slopping out and cleaning urinals. It helped. My fists stayed unclenched, but my body was stretched so taut that I knew it might snap at any moment.

'Why did you do it, Gus? Don't you think you owe me some kind of explanation,' I added when he hesitated.

'I suppose I do.' He couldn't resist the chance to show off. He continued, 'When I saw Vanessa quite by chance here on the Island I knew that I was still in love with her, but she told me she was happily married and could never leave you. After that I made it my business to find out everything I could about you. You valued honesty; you were creative and enterprising. You'd built up a successful business. Vanessa was loyal to you, a dedicated wife and mother. She hated hypocrisy and deceit. She had rejected me once; I wasn't about to lose her for the second time. I knew that the only way to get her to love and marry me was if I disgraced you. I had to show her you were a sham.'

'And that's when you decided you had to ruin me and that Vanessa would need a big strong shoulder to cry on.' Even if I had tried I wouldn't have been able to keep the bitterness from my voice. I could see in an instance that Gus liked that. It gave him back an element of dominance. OK, so let him think that.

'Family history is a hobby of mine,' he said. 'I started to delve into yours. Everyone has skeletons in their cupboard and I surmised that your family would be no exception.'

I recalled seeing the framed picture of Gus's genealogy on the wall in his breakfast room. The same room that my sons had sat in and done their homework. For a moment I thought fury might invade my calm and erupt into physical violence. I willed myself to be still. It wasn't time yet.

'What I did find out was quite remarkable,' Gus said. 'Your grandfather had drowned in August 1940, not long after the attack on the Ventnor radar station.'

I didn't correct him, but let him continue.

'That was my starting point. I found Percy who, as you know, always liked to talk about the war. Soon I had the story of the three young men, Hugo, Max and Edward. Percy wouldn't say what happened to the others. I could see he was uncomfortable about something so I made my own enquiries and learnt that Hugo had been

arrested for treason, after being turned in by two
teenagers. He had died in prison before he could
be hanged. I tracked down his wife, Amelia, who
had a daughter and a grandson: Miles Wolverton.
I didn't approach him, not then. Later on I
located Maximilian Weber. He was a professor
at Frankfurt University. I was surprised you'd
not followed it up before.'

'What did Max tell you?' I snapped.

'Everything. He had no choice. I threatened to
expose him. I told him I was from the British
Government. He was old and he was ill. It didn't
take much and perhaps he wanted it off his
conscience anyway. He told me about the money
they had taken from the Jews in payment for
helping them to escape Germany, and that Hugo
had been a spy. I knew he was lying. After all
why Hugo when Max was German. After that it
was easy. I went to Miles and told him that your
mother had betrayed his grandfather. She had
helped to destroy Hugo's reputation. I said that
Hugo had suffered terribly in prison and the
authorities had hushed up his death. Miles
couldn't get a pardon without raking up the past
but he could get even with you. I told him about
my idea of the fictitious charity and that we could
make some money from it. I needed three

wealthy businessmen to cough up. Miles could supply that easily. The connection with my firm was a coincidence and I hadn't realised it until you crashed in on me in Guernsey. Miles really enjoyed watching you suffer the humiliations of the trial and imprisonment. He saw it as justice.'

I tensed. Was he goading me deliberately? No. As I stared at him I saw how mad he was. What a lethal combination he and Miles had made. Miles eaten up with an inferiority complex and fuelled by revenge, and Gus suffused with a surfeit of unhealthy superiority. To them I had been merely an instrument to achieve what they wanted. Well fuck them! One of them was dead. Prison though would be better than death for Gus Newberry. But I wasn't finished yet.

'How did you find out about the brooches?' I asked almost casually, marvelling at my ability to disguise my real emotion. But then prison had taught me so much, and in that instance I knew with certainty I could never go back to being the Alex Albury I had once been.

'What brooches?' Gus said.

'You didn't know that each man had part of an account number engraved on the back of a brooch which gave the whereabouts of the Jewish money?'

'No. Does Miles know?'

'He did. He had all three brooches before he died. We had a little accident in my boat. They're somewhere at the bottom of the Solent now.' Or were they? Perhaps the police had discovered them on Miles's body. Crowder hadn't said.

Gus went on, 'Now I can see why Miles got so fanatical about you. He killed Joe.'

'I know and others. Did he kill Couldner?'

'Someone had to. It was the only way to get the police to start the enquiry. I haven't killed anyone, Alex.'

'Only me and everything I valued,' I said. My pulse was quickening and I was fighting to keep myself under control. There was silence for a moment. With every last fibre of my being I urged myself to remain calm.

I crossed to the patio doors. I thought of Vanessa. Gus had tricked and betrayed her as much as he had me. I knew that she would never forgive me for what I was about to do to Gus, but that couldn't be helped. Besides I didn't want her forgiveness now.

I turned back. 'Why did you pay Rowde to say he would hurt my sons?'

'After you showed up at the house I could see that Vanessa was eaten up with guilt. I couldn't have that. It would poison our relationship. So Miles found Rowde for me. He told Rowde that you had confessed to him that you really had stolen the three million and that you knew exactly where it was. Rowde found Westnam. I told him, through Miles, where to look. I'd kept tabs on him. The one way to get to the money you had was through your family. So Rowde threatened you. Then he was paid to say he had kidnapped them. He was also to get a bonus when the three million was found which was to be shared three ways between him, Miles and me, only he didn't know my identity. Everything was arranged through Miles. Instead I flew Vanessa and the boys here, the day after you and I returned from Guernsey. I thought you might kill Rowde for me, which would have been convenient.'

'I might still do that,' I said evenly.

Gus sat up surprised. 'Why?'

'For three million pounds. I'll go ahead just as we planned. I'll fly with him to Zurich on Monday. He calls Vanessa when we get there, I speak to her and then you call me to say that they've been released. Rowde will believe it. I'll get the money and then I'll kill Rowde.'

'How?'

'Do you really want to know?' There was a silence. After a moment I continued. 'Prison

teaches you all sorts of tricks, including how to
kill a man. I'll do it on one condition. I get to
keep the three million. I deserve some kind of
compensation. I think I've more than earned it,
don't you?'

'And you'll go away and stay away.'

I nodded.

'You won't have any further claim on Vanessa
or your sons?'

'No. If my sons decide to come looking for
me when they're older then that's up to them,
though I doubt they'll find me. Look, Gus, I'm
tired. I've got nothing to keep me here. This way
I can start a new life for myself, away from here
and all my memories. You've got what you want,
Vanessa and a family, and I've got some kind of
compensation for what I've suffered, and a
chance to start afresh without psychos like
Rowde on my back.'

Gus scrutinised me for a moment thinking
over my words. 'OK, it's a deal.'

'Right, tell me how and where I can find the
money.' I saw him hesitate. 'I've got to know,
Gus, otherwise I'll call the police and tell them
everything. They'll start an investigation…'

'It's in a Swiss numbered account in the Zurich
International Bank. I'll need to call them and tell

them you're coming. I'll authorise them to hand the money over to you.'

'I'll be travelling on a false passport. I'll call you and give you the details as soon as I get them from Rowde, OK?'

Gus nodded.

'Let me have the number now, Gus.'

He hesitated, shrugged and then took a business card from his wallet and wrote twelve numbers on it. I recognised part of it (even though it was jumbled up) as Vanessa's birth date.

'How do I know this is the real number and not a fake?'

'How do I know you'll kill Rowde and stay away from Vanessa and the boys?'

I nodded. 'OK.'

'Are you sure you can handle Rowde?'

'Yes.'

He glanced at his watch. 'I'll need to make some arrangements.'

As soon as he'd gone I stuffed a pillow in my bed and stepped onto the aft deck, closing the patio doors behind me. I had to keep alert, but I was exhausted both mentally and physically. I snatched a glance at my watch: it was almost 5.30am. The night was moonless and pitch dark. I shivered in the wind and rain, thinking that at least the cold would prevent me from falling asleep, and I didn't think I would have long to wait, correctly as it turned out. A noise alerted me. I crouched down out of sight. A shadowy figure was moving around inside the lounge, and then disappeared from my view. After a moment I heard it step off the houseboat and I dropped down onto the shore and ran after it along the Embankment. I reached him just as he was about to climb into a car.

'Good try, Gus, but I'm still alive.' He spun round. The hood slipped from his head.

'But not for long.'

He swung the petrol can. I saw it coming and dodged out of the way. I reached out and grabbed him around the legs. He fell down thrashing about. I lifted his head and bashed it against the hard earth, then I balled my fist and smashed it into his face, once, twice.

'And this one's for my mother.' I hit him again. 'And for Ruby.'

Then four men in dark clothes appeared from nowhere. Two were pulling me off and restraining me. I tried to shake them off. It took a command from Crowder before they released me.

'Call an ambulance,' Crowder addressed his sergeant, 'And get an officer to accompany Mr Newberry to St Mary's Hospital.'

Crowder's eyes travelled beyond me and his mobile was pressed to his ear.

I turned knowing what I would see. Flames were licking out of the houseboat.

'Don't worry, Alex. We got your conversation with Mr Newberry. Have you got the code to the Swiss bank account?'

I handed over the card Gus had given me. 'It's the correct number only Gus didn't expect me to live long enough to collect the money.'

'This money of your grandfather's – any idea of the code?'

'No.' So the brooches hadn't been discovered on Miles's body.

'Don't you think it should go back to those who it belongs to?'

I did but finding who that was, was a whole new ballgame. 'Maybe one day it will,' I said, thinking of those birth dates.

'Do you want a lift anywhere?'

'No.'

I watched Crowder and the ambulance drive away. Vanessa was going to get a shock. I hoped the boys would be all right and weather it though. Maybe they could stay with me for a while, but where, I thought, walking slowly back to my burning houseboat. The fire fighters were doing a good job, but I didn't think there would be much left.

The commotion had attracted my neighbour. Scarlett was standing in the roadside opposite, staring anxiously at the burning spectacle. I hoped the police had told her there was no one inside. Maybe she wouldn't care if I was after what I had done to her mother. But the relief on her face as she swung round and saw me lifted my heart and filled me with hope. After all the deceptions I wondered if I could trust again, but with Scarlett I knew that what you saw was what you got.

'Well you might have told me that you were OK,' she cried, exasperated. She was as dishevelled as always, wearing her long green raincoat over a T-shirt and shorts with her big boots on her feet, but her hair was brown and all one colour. I wondered if that augured well.

'I'm sorry about Ruby. I tried to save her.'

Sadness touched her face. 'I know, and nearly got yourself killed in the process. The lifeboat men told me. It wasn't your fault, Alex. She's at peace now.'

Relief overwhelmed me. She didn't blame me. She stretched out a hand and I clasped it tightly. We stood for a moment in silence staring at the smouldering ruin of my houseboat. The fire fighters were dampening it down now. The wind had eased back and it had stopped raining. Slowly the day was coming alive. Scarlett shivered and I drew my arm around her.

'You'll want somewhere to stay,' she said.

'Are you offering?'

'Only if you don't mind a bit of mess and can make a mean cup of tea.'

I smiled. 'Try me.'

'No time like the present.'

We crossed the road but before we stepped onto her houseboat she turned to face me.

'Is it over now, Alex?' she said, quietly.

I looked across at what was left of my houseboat then back into her sad brown eyes. I thought of everything that had happened to me and what was still to come: Gus's trial and Vanessa's anguish. But the burden of proving my innocence had lifted from my shoulders, and the hard knot of anger and revenge inside me had vanished.

'Yes, Scarlett,' I replied, steadily. 'It's over.'

BY THE SAME AUTHOR

# TIDE OF DEATH

### A MARINE MYSTERY FEATURING
### DI ANDY HORTON
### AND BARNEY CANTELLI

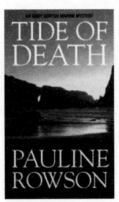

It is DI Andy Horton's second day back in Portsmouth CID after being suspended for eight months. Whilst out running in the early morning he trips over the naked battered body of a man on the beach. PC Evans has been stabbed the night before, the DCI is up before a promotion board and Sergeant Cantelli is having trouble with his fifteen-year-old daughter. But Horton's mind is on other things not least of which is trying to prove his innocence after being accused of rape.

Beset by personal problems and aided by Cantelli, Horton sets out to find a killer who will stop at nothing to cover his tracks. As he gets closer to the truth, he risks not only his career but also his life…

*'Be prepared to be taken aback!'*

ISBN 0955098203    Paperback    £6.99

BY THE SAME AUTHOR

# IN COLD DAYLIGHT

## A GRIPPING
## MARINE MYSTERY

Fire fighter Jack Bartholomew dies whilst trying to put out a fire in a derelict building. Was it an accident or arson? Marine artist Adam Greene doesn't know, only that he has lost his closest friend. He attends the funeral ready to mourn his friend only to find that another funeral intrudes upon his thoughts and one he's tried hard to forget for the last fifteen years. But before he has time to digest this, or discover the identity of the stranger stalking him, Jack's house is ransacked.

Unaware of the risks he is running, Adam soon finds himself caught up in a mysterious and dangerous web of deceit. By exposing a secret that has lain dormant for years Adam is forced to face his own dark secrets and, as the facts reveal themselves, the prospects for his survival look bleak. But Adam knows there is no turning back; he has to get to the truth no matter what the cost, even if it means his life.

*'Plenty of twists and turns. A thoroughly enjoyable read.'*

ISBN 0955098211    Paperback    £6.99

Coming soon:

**Deadly Harbour**
*– An Andy Horton Marine Mystery*

*www.rowmark.co.uk*